A PARANORMAL MYSTERY THRILLER

GHOST GIRL GONE

BOOKS ONE TO THREE

SIMON B. MURIK

Ghost Girl Gone
A Paranormal Mystery Thriller

Simon B. Murik

Published by:
Paranormal Publishing
www.ParanormalPublishing.net

ISBN: 978-0-9971185-4-4

OTHER BOOKS AVAILABLE FROM PARANORMAL PUBLISHING

True Ghost Stories and Hauntings

Chilling Stories of Poltergeists, Unexplained
Phenomenon, and Haunted Houses

Volumes I, II, III, IV, V, and Boxed Set of Volumes 1-III.

Ghost Girl Gone

A Paranormal Mystery Thriller, Books One,
Two, Three, and the Boxed Set.

For kids: *Ghost Coloring Book*

Kids love coloring these ghosts as they bring them to life
and have lots of fun with this spooky activity book!

BONUS FOR READERS OF THIS BOOK

Get 3 FREE ghost stories at
www.paranormalpublishing.com/ghoststories

CONTENTS

BOOK ONE

I smiled as Elyse ran down the beach as the waves broke against the shoreline. She jumped into the air and then did a cartwheel when she landed on the golden sand. Her laughter carried through the warm sea air as she ran farther and farther until she was just a happy silhouette in the distance. I called for her to come back but she kept going. About a hundred yards out in the ocean, a wave a good fifty or sixty feet high rose out of the water and started to rush towards her. I yelled Elyse's name as loud as I could and my voice echoed across the entire beach like I was in some kind of exotic echo chamber. Elyse stopped and turned around with a grin that sparkled across the beach like a diamond. She waved at me. I pointed to the monstrous wave heading towards her and yelled for her to come back. Elyse either couldn't hear me or wasn't listening because she started dancing and spinning down the beach again.

And a second later the wave crashed down on her and she was gone forever.

* * *

My eyes popped open with my forehead pressed against the steering wheel. A warm tongue licked my face but my mind was a cold, dark blank. A violent image of swerving off the road and crashing into a tree rushed into my head and I felt like a bolt of electricity had shot through me.

"Elyse!" I yelled as I spun towards the passenger seat, sending our yellow lab, Oscar, stumbling into the back seat and interrupting his procedure of reviving me with his tongue.

My daughter wasn't there.

I snapped the seatbelt off and turned towards the back seat. Oscar was the only one back there and I popped the car door open and stepped onto the swerving country road. Oscar jumped out of the car and put his paws onto my legs with his eyes wide. I scratched the back of his head and stared down the road as it twisted through the thick, green trees into the gray distance. I then hurried through the damp Oregon air to the other side of the car.

Nothing but thick green grass leading up to dense pine tree forest.

Elyse had been buckled in tight and the windows weren't broken so there was no way she'd been thrown out of the car—maybe she'd gone to get help?

I went back to the middle of the road and looked it both directions. "Elyse!" I yelled. Her name echoed through the air loudly enough that anyone within a half mile could hear it but my gut told me that no one did. I ran my hands through my sweaty hair and looked at the car. The front of it was smashed into the tree like a shredded metal "U"—the thing wasn't going anywhere.

I slid my phone out of my pocket and hit Elyse's number. There was a ring and then the phone went dead. I checked the screen—zero signal bars. *Damn it.* But it wasn't surprising. We were in the middle of nowhere Oregon, which had been the point of the whole trip. Take a few days to try and bond with a daughter who'd grown more and more detached from me every day since her mother had been killed in a car accident.

I rubbed my face as dread moved through my body like sludge. Oscar leaned against my leg and I thought about seeing Nicole's burnt and broken body in the wreckage.

I also knew it'd been no accident.

The same people who'd set me up for embezzlement had taken her out as payback for me going to the cops.

Not that the cops had believed me—or anyone else for that matter.

And here I was now. A missing daughter, a smashed car, and a dead phone. My heart beat hard and my stomach felt like I'd eaten a plate of rotten oysters.

My ears perked up at the rumbling of what sounded like a truck beyond the trees from the direction we'd come from.

A few seconds later a red pickup rolled around the bend and I waved at it. The truck flashed its lights and began to slow. As it got closer, I saw a thick-necked man with wavy gray hair and scruffy beard driving it. The pickup crept up next to me and I went around to the driver's side. The window was down and I got hit with a strong whiff of cherry tobacco.

"Got some trouble?" the man asked.

"Yeah, I do. I swerved off the road to miss hitting a deer and the next thing I knew I woke up with my daughter missing and my car wrapped around a tree."

"Oh, boy," he said. "Yeah, the damn deer are all over the place now. You try calling her?"

"Yeah, no signal."

He shook his head and his eyes went down a bit. "Yeah, it can be hard to get a good signal out here. Real hard. Just a lot of interference sometimes …" He looked back at me. "Well if you're OK leaving the car, I can take you over to Gold Pine. It's only a couple of miles from here and you can talk to the sheriff about your daughter. You could probably get a tow truck out here also."

"Yeah, I hate to inconvenience you, but I would really appreciate that," I said as I looked up and down the road again. "I just don't know. If my daughter comes back here …"

The guy's eyes dropped a bit again like it was a sign he was getting hit by a heavy thought. He shook his head. "How long do you think you were out for?"

"I don't know. Could have been an hour, maybe even two."

"I doubt she's coming back here then," he said. "I would just get over to that sheriff's as fast as possible if I were you."

"Yeah, you might be right." A cold sweat had broken out over my back. The daze of the crash had worn off and it was sinking in real hard that Elyse was gone.

"I'll tell you, you don't want to waste more time. I would get over to the sheriff's," the man repeated.

"Yeah, let's do that," I said as I gazed at the thick pines that lined the forest.

"All right, hop in and I'll take you over there."

I went around the truck with Oscar pressed alongside me and grabbed my leather overnight bag out of my car along with Oscar's food and treats. I unzipped the bag and put Oscar's things in there, then zipped it back up, opened the truck door, and climbed in. Oscar jumped all the way from the grass onto my lap and scrambled into the back of the cab.

"Name's J.T.," the man said, holding out a thick, calloused hand that looked like it could crush a cue ball into dust.

"Ryan," I said and shook it.

J.T. threw the truck into drive and we headed off.

I squinted as the warm September wind blew against my face and my knee shook up and down at the thought of Elyse coming back to the car with me not there.

"If ya don't mind me asking, what were you and your daughter doing up this way?" J.T. asked as we sped past a sand-colored, jagged rocked canyon that looked like it ran a few hundred feet deep.

"Just a little road trip," I said. "Her mother was killed in a car accident a couple of years ago and things have been a touch frosty between us since."

"Ah, sorry to hear that," J.T. said. "I lost my wife, too, a few years ago. Life has a twisted way of doing things."

I nodded and stared out as the canyon faded in the distance. "Yes it does."

We drove the next few minutes in silence and as we rounded a bend, a big blue sign with a white mountain on it and a sun shining golden light onto thick pine trees at its base popped up at the side of the road.

WELCOME TO GOLD PINE
"The Best Kept Secret In Oregon"

"Gold Pine," I said.

"Yep. Nice little town. You'll get the help you need here," he said. His voice trailed off almost like he'd swallowed a hard candy when he'd said "here."

I looked at J.T.; he shot me a glance and then his eyes went right back to the road. We veered right and I could see what looked like shops and two- and three-story buildings stretched out in front of a four- or five-thousand foot white rock mountain about a half mile away.

"Wow," I said.

"Yeah, she's sort of a hidden gem. Occasionally you see the town pop up in those 'best one-hundred places to live' lists, but they've kept it pretty quiet. Maybe six or seven hundred residents."

We drove into the town and midway through the first block, J.T. pulled the car up to the curb. I looked out at a set of wide stone steps leading to a gray concrete building with a pair of bronze doors between a couple of wide, tinted windows. *Gold Pine Sheriff's Department.* "Here you go, my friend. Sheriff Eastman will help you find your little girl from here."

"Thanks for your help, J.T.," I said, holding my hand out. "Seriously, I don't know what I would have done …"

J.T. took my hand and held it firm. "Good luck, Ryan. I hope you find your daughter." I started to take my hand away but his grip tightened, "Just remember this:

Gold Pine is a good town with good people. People who come here live a nice life. But," he leaned in so that the smell of tobacco was so strong I could almost taste it, "it's also a lonely town—you know what I mean?"

I didn't know what he meant but his strong-jawed face stayed set like stone for a second and I wondered if there was something more he wanted to tell me. He didn't, though, and he let my hand go. I looked back out at the town. J.T. had seemed normal enough until his spooky little warning—but what was normal anymore anyways? "Thanks, J.T. I will." I got out of the truck and Oscar hopped out after me. He gave me a single bark and I scratched the back of his head. When I looked back up, J.T.'s truck was already out of sight.

I took a deep breath and looked at the town. It was caught somewhere between modern and old. Starbucks, a 50s-style movie theater with neon-striped marquee, random shops with chatting women carrying white-handled shopping bags bustling in and out of them. It'd actually probably be a nice place to spend a couple of days but my only interest was getting to that sheriff. I jogged up the steps of the building with Oscar trailing me and I took the treats out of my bag, gave him one, and told him to wait. He sat down on the pavement and I pushed the door open and stepped into a marble-floored waiting room with a couple of leather chairs set against the plain white wall. To my right, a dark-haired woman with a sharp chin and tan skin sat a glass-topped desk staring at a computer screen. Her name plate said "Lori." A black-and-white framed photo of the town hung on the wall behind her.

As I walked past the wall to the desk, I could see the rest of the station. A pair of offices lined the left side of the station while a plexiglass jail cell was built into the opposite side. The woman looked away from the computer and smiled. "Can I help you?" she asked.

"Yes, you can," I said as I set my hands on the desk. "My daughter is missing and I was told I should see Sheriff Eastman."

"Oh," she said as she placed her hand on her chest. "Let me just go check his office." She got up and walked to the first office; she stepped inside and a few seconds later came back out and waved me over.

I walked over to her. A bald man who looked like he could throw a shot put a mile and a half with skin like sun-beaten leather sat at a paper-covered desk. He gestured at the chair in front of the desk and I walked in and sat down.

"I'm Sheriff Eastman," he said, holding his heavy hand across the desk, "Tell me what happened."

I shook his hand and I did. When I was done the sheriff gave a small nod and picked up the phone.

"Hello, is this Tony? OK, good. This is Sheriff Eastman over in Gold Pine. I wanted to let you guys know over there to be on the look out for a possibly lost or abducted twelve-year-old girl. Her name is Elyse Walker. She's 5'0", 105 lbs, sandy hair, blue eyes. Yeah, you can call my private line. Yes, anytime, day or night. OK, great. Thank you."

Eastman hung up the phone. "That was the sheriff's office in Jessup's Peak. It's a small town about thirty miles from where you crashed. After that it's another hour before you get anywhere with electricity. Do you have a place to stay tonight?"

"I don't."

"OK, what I'd suggest is that you go down to the Mountain View Hotel at the edge of Main Street. Clare should be working the desk right now, tell her what happened and that I sent you and ask if she has a room available. She should put you up at no charge. If she has any questions tell her to call me."

"Thanks, this is just ..." I couldn't even finish the thought.

"Believe me, I understand, Mr. Walker. A missing daughter is about as difficult as it gets and I'm going to do everything possible to make sure she's brought back safe and sound. This is a very safe town and so is Jessup's Peak. Mostly likely she wandered off after the accident to try and get help and just got lost. So we're going to find her. But until then—and I know this is hard—please try to relax. I'll be in touch as soon as I find anything out. If you don't hear from me in the next twenty-four hours please call me and I'll give you whatever information I have."

The sheriff slid a card out of his shirt pocket and handed it to me. It had both his office number and his cell number. "Thanks, Sheriff," I said as I got up and walked back to the lobby. I gave Lori a nod as I headed to the door. When I got to it I pushed it open and squinted as the surprising sunlight hit my eyes. Oscar bounced to his feet with a big tongue-wagging smile and I scratched under his chin. "Come on, Oscar. Let's check out the hotel and get you some water."

I walked down the steps and back onto the sidewalk. It was just after three and the sun shone brightly through the thinning gray sky like it was making up for being covered up for most of the day. The street wasn't crowded, but it was active. Men on cell phones and women with their kids gabbed and laughed as I passed Max's Drug Store, a pet store called Paw's with crates of wide-eyed puppy dogs and sleepy-eyed cats lined up against the window, and a frozen yogurt shop with a couple of eight- or nine-year-olds sitting at a table smearing vanilla and chocolate yogurt on their faces. After that was an Irish Pub called O'Mally's. The front of the place was green-

and-yellow painted brick with an outdoor patio filled with people eating thick sandwiches and sipping stouts. Elyse being gone made me too guilty to be hungry but I hadn't eaten in five hours. Maybe I'd come back here after I checked in.

As I moved past the restaurant, I could see across the street, through the space between Joe's Sporting Goods and a women's clothing store called Her Stuff, the gray tombstones of a small cemetery set about a quarter mile in the distance beyond a street of homes in the residential area. My spine chilled as I imagined Elyse laying on the ground somewhere and I forced my eyes ahead again. A five-story red brick building with a sign that said "Mountain View Hotel" in big gold letters on the front of it stood a half block away on my right. As I walked to it, I looked over at what might have been an abandoned warehouse across the street. The door was dead bolted and through the big windows that wrapped around the building it was just empty space.

I came up to the hotel, pushed the door open, and stepped inside. Oscar trotted ahead of me and strode right towards a blonde woman with sparkling green eyes and perky dimples standing behind a cherrywood counter with one of those old-fashioned-looking gold desk lamps with the little chain hanging on it that you pull to turn it on and off. She grinned and waved at Oscar and then smiled at me. "How are you today?" she asked.

"Um, *I'm OK*. Are you Clare?" I asked.

"Why yes, I am," she said with her face still stuck in perma-smile.

"Hi, Clare. My name is Ryan and I just came from the sheriff's office."

The smile vanished as her face tightened.

I then proceeded to tell her about the situation and she nodded intensely as I spoke. "And so Sheriff Eastman told me that I might be able to stay here tonight no charge," I said.

"Yes, *absolutely*. And I'm so sorry to hear this. I'm going to give you room 417 and *please* let me know if there's anything you need."

She reached down and her hand came up with a clipboard that she set on the desk. "If you could just sign in here, I can give you your room key."

I signed the sheet with the pen attached to the counter and she set the keycard down. I took the card, thanked her, and then carried my bag to the open elevator as Oscar followed me. I stepped inside and pressed four. My head felt warm and my hands went cold as the door closed. Oscar looked up at me and whimpered. I scratched under his chin, "I know, buddy, I know," I said quietly.

When the door slid back open I stepped into a gray-carpeted hall with beige walls and a floor-to-ceiling window at the end of the hall showing the mountain. I walked down the hall and after a few doors came to room 417 on my left. I slid the card into the reader; the door clicked open and I turned the knob and walked in.

A queen-sized bed made tightly and smoothly, a dresser across from it with a silver flat-panel TV, and tan carpeting. Through the window on the opposite side of the room I could see the abandoned-looking building across the street. I walked up to it and peered out. It was almost four now and the afternoon sun had really broken through, covering the street and shops with hazy, orange-yellow light. I wanted to call the sheriff to see if he'd found anything but I knew it'd be pointless. He'd call me when he had any info. Oscar put his paws up on the window and looked out with me.

My muscles felt hollow and weak and even though I still wasn't hungry, I figured I'd better get something to eat. Sitting alone in the room wouldn't do me any good anyways. I went back into the hallway and headed down to the lobby. Clare's mouth widened into a closed mouth "I feel so sorry for you" smile when she saw me and I nodded at her as I went back outside.

The street was busier now and families bustled back and forth with kids chasing each other in circles. Some pretty nice cars were now lined up in the parking spots along the street. Porsches, Mercedes, a few Corvettes— even some expensive-looking black and chrome Harleys.

I headed over to the pub and when I got there I asked the bouncy twenty-something-year-old hostess for a table on the patio. She smiled and said "of course" like I'd asked her if she wanted a free trip to Aruba and led me out to a two-person table right next to the fence around the patio. A blonde waitress with a happy, full face almost like a smiling cantaloupe appeared almost as soon as the girl left.

"Hi there. Can I start you off with something to drink?" she asked.

I said nothing for a second and then caved. "Sure, do you have any type of Hefeweizen?"

"Yep. It's our own micro-brew," she said.

I bit my lower lip. It didn't seem right to have a drink, but if I could just take a bit of the edge off … "All right, I'll go with one," I said.

"Great, I'll go get that for you," she said and hurried off.

I checked my phone—no call, no texts, nothing. I tapped my fingers against the table and waited for the beer. While I waited, I suddenly realized I hadn't done anything about getting the car towed. I sighed and figured it didn't really matter anyways. The car just didn't seem important right now and I could take care of it tomorrow.

A couple of boys riding bikes appeared on the other side of the street and I watched as they glided around cars and people with an ease that only a carefree kid could pull off. A glass being set it front of me on the table snapped me out of my daze. I looked over to see that the waitress had also brought a bowl of water for Oscar.

"Oh, great. Thanks a lot," I said as I took a couple of Milk-Bones out of my pocket and dropped them on the ground. Oscar munched on the bones as I took a drink and stared at my dark phone screen.

"What a beautiful dog," said a smooth, feminine voice that made me think of a late-night DJ who played music for people who met in bars to hook up to. I looked up and saw a woman with long, black hair, big, almond eyes, and legs that a professional runway model would be jealous of petting Oscar.

Normally my heart would have started to race but my missing daughter had turned it into a piece of lead. "Thanks," I said.

"I'm sorry; I'm Tara," she said, holding out a hand with long, dark-green painted nails that could have been an exhibit in an art store.

"Ryan," I said as I shook it. As she was passing by the table with a pitcher of water, my happy server saw Tara and stopped.

"Hi, will you be joining him?" she asked.

Tara looked at me and I semi-shrugged and tilted my head as I looked down the street again. "Yeah, sure, sit down."

Tara sat down. "I'll have a glass of Pinot Grigio."

The girl looked at me. I still had half my beer left. "I'm fine right now. Thanks."

Tara ran her hand through her hair and flashed a big smile. "So I take it you're just visiting our little town?"

I nodded. "Yeah, was on a road trip with my daughter. And … well, she disappeared a couple miles outside of here," I said. I took a sip of beer and scratched behind Oscar's ears.

The woman's eyes went wide. "I'm so sorry!"

"Thanks. Yeah, I don't really have words for it."

"Did you report it to the sheriff?"

"Yes—I did it as soon as I got here a couple of hours ago."

"How did it happen?" she asked.

As I told her the story, her eyes got wider and wider and she pressed her hand against the side of her face like she needed to brace it from falling over.

The waitress brought the wine.

Tara took a sip. "So do you have a place to stay tonight?"

"Yeah, I've got a room at the Mountain View."

She nodded and watched me as I finished my beer. "So what do you do?" I asked. I hated the "what do you do?" question but it was all I could muster right now.

"I'm an attorney. My office is just down the street; you probably walked past it before."

"How long have you been here?"

"Just over three years. It's a nice place to live," she said, gazing over my head. "One of my goals is to scale the mountain before I leave."

"You're kidding," I said.

"Nope. Got into rock climbing at the gym I belonged to in Chicago and when I discovered this place I became fascinated with the idea of climbing the mountain."

A couple of guys wearing Ray Bans sat down at the table next to us. The wiry one with short blond hair in khakis and a sky-blue Polo shirt waved the waitress over as soon as he sat down while the beefier, black-haired guy in faded jeans and a black, short-sleeved v-neck gave Tara a good look-over.

Tara just sipped her wine and stared off at the mountain, either not noticing or caring that some guy was checking her out.

"Would you like another beer?"

I looked over to see our server, the happy cantaloupe, beaming over us. "Sure, I'll have one more," I said, a little unnerved with how quickly I said it.

"Ms.? Another Grigio?"

"Yes, please," Tara said with her eyes still on the mountain.

Cantaloupe girl hustled off.

"So is your wife here with you?" Tara asked.

I shook my head and rubbed the back of my neck. "No. My wife, Nicole, was killed in a car accident two years ago."

"Wow. Again, I'm so sorry."

The girl returned and set our drinks on the table. I took a sip—sthe stuff was strong, six or seven percent alcohol at least—and rubbed my chin. "The truth is she didn't just die though."

Tara's eyes widened again.

Thanks to the beer, the words were coming out a little too easy now, but I flowed into the story. "About four years ago I got involved with some hedge fund guys who wanted me to run an embezzlement scam for about three million with the firm I was with. I said no, and ended up getting set up anyways. I got sentenced to three years and got out after twelve months. A couple weeks later the brakes on my wife's car went out and she smashed into a cement truck while going eighty miles an hour on the highway." I took a drink and watched as a raven landed on the sidewalk. "The police said she was killed on impact." The bird stared at me for a second and then took off again.

Tara said nothing. Her eyes actually reminded me of Lisa's. Not the color, but the expression. Sympathetic and questioning at the same time. Her phone beeped and she checked it.

"Well, I hate to do this but I have a client I need to meet with at my office," she said.

"Oh, OK. No problem," I said. I was pretty much out of conversation anyways—with a missing daughter it's hard to make small talk.

Tara reached into her purse and took her wallet out. She opened it up. "I'm going to give you my card. I know we just met, but please let me know while you're in town if you hear anything about your daughter and if I can do anything to help." She slid out a business card and set it on the table. I picked it up.

Tara Carlyle - Attorney at Law

"Oh, thank you. I appreciate that," I said. "And I will let you know if I hear anything."

She finished her wine and started to take out some money.

"That's OK, I've got it," I said.

"Are you sure? Please, I—"

"No, don't worry about it. I appreciated the chat—helped me get out of my head a bit," I said.

"OK, well thank you for the drink. And again, *please* let me know when you find something out."

"I will," I said. Maybe I would, maybe I wouldn't. She might have been great looking but I didn't know her from the man on the moon.

Tara left and I went back to my beer. The sun had dipped into a big orange fireball and it lit the street in an intense blood-orange glow. I ended up ordering a steak, and thanks to Oscar's persistent staring at me, I shared about a third of it with him.

When I was done, music had started to play in the pub and the patio was filled with happy, chatting locals in expensive-looking jeans and either more Polo shirts or the kind of artsy t-shirts that send you into mild shock when you check the price.

The scene was too much for me and I waved my server down as she darted between tables with drinks. I paid the bill, left her a fifty-percent tip for karma, and got out of there. It was almost six now and I was still too restless to go back to the hotel. I crossed the street and gazed through the store windows. When I passed a music shop with a couple of black baby grands in the window, my heart sank. Elyse had gotten really good at the piano during the past year.

For the next few minutes I just put one foot in front of the other without paying attention to anything. If it wasn't for Oscar brushing up against my leg, I'm not sure I would have felt anything either. Maybe it was because it was getting darker now, but Elyse being out there alone—or maybe not alone—gave my gut a feeling like rubbing alcohol had burned my insides away. There was no emotional pain, just emptiness—hell, pain would have been an improvement.

As I got to a little hamburger place at the street corner, I saw a stone path that ran up through the field of grass that separated the downtown area from the side streets of residential homes. When I got to it, I saw that it cut across the field to the strip of homes—and beyond the homes I saw the cemetery again under the now purple-blue sky.

Without thinking about it, I followed the path to the cemetery.

A waist-high iron gate wrapped around the cemetery with the open entrance right in front of me. Another raven suddenly landed on the fence—hell, it could have been the same one as before for all I knew. It again stared at me for a few seconds and then flew off towards town. I looked at Oscar who had lain down and buried his face in his paws.

"Don't ask me why, but we're going in there, Oscar."

Oscar pushed himself to his feet slower than usual.

I walked through the gate as Oscar's paws padded against the path and started looking over the tombstones. A lot of the names on the stones were of people born in the 1920s or 30s. I passed one guy who'd made it from 1902 to 2003 and a woman who'd gone all the way from 1907 to 2010.

And then I saw this:

In Loving Memory
of
Jessica Ray
2002 - 2013

Basically the same age as Elyse. My throat choked up but I held the tears back. *First Nicole and now this.*

"Let's get out of here, Oscar," I said.

I turned around and started walking back up the path to town. When I got there the street was a lot quieter. The storefront lights were on and noise and music came from the pub, but there were only a few people at the far end of the street shuffling about. I headed towards the hotel and when I got to the corner of the abandoned building, I was about to cross over to the hotel when I heard what sounded like a young girl crying from inside the building. The crying seemed to sweep along the windows of the building almost like a sheet of water flowing over them and as I took a few steps closer the crying got louder.

I walked to the front of the building and put my hands on my hips. The single iron door looked like it could stop a bazooka blast, but as I walked up to it, I heard the crying so clearly it was almost like the door was made of thin cardboard. There was no point, but for some reason I reached for the door anyways. An inch away from the handle my hand suddenly felt cold and moist—like it'd gotten stuck in slushy ice water. Pulling my hand back, I stepped away from the door and walked to the side of the building. I went up to the first window and peered through. The crying sound pressed against the glass like it was trying to push its way through.

But there was nothing inside. Just unfurnished space.

I walked towards the back of the building and Oscar whimpered. I had a clear view of the cemetery from here and my back muscles shivered a bit. The crying seemed to follow me as I walked. It sounded close and faraway at the same time and I looked through another window but still couldn't see anyone or anything. A blast of cold wind knocked me back a step and the crying seemed to get swept away in it.

Was my mind just going haywire from the stress, the beer, being overtired?

I rounded the next corner of the building and the crying came back. I stepped up to the window and looked through again.

Nothing.

Oscar howled and my heart felt like a ten pound bowling ball.

It was time to get some rest.

We walked back to the sidewalk and crossed the street. The "Mountain View Hotel" sign was lit in yellow light, giving the red bricks of the building and part of the street a warm glow. When I got to the entrance, I pulled the door open and walked in with Oscar behind me.

Clare was still at the desk and she managed a strained smile. "Hi, Mr. Walker," she said.

"How you doing, Clare?" I said as I gave her a nod and the best happy face I could muster. I started to walk towards the elevator and then stopped and turned around.

"Do you by chance know much about the building across the street?" I asked.

Clare set the pen down. "I know a little bit," she said. "It's basically a warehouse. I don't think it's been used in years."

I rubbed my hands together. "Is that it?"

"Yeah, pretty much," Clare said.

I looked at her for a second and then nodded.

"OK, thanks, Clare. I'm going to head up."

"My pleasure, Mr. Walker. I'll be here until one so feel free to let me know if you need anything."

I needed a Valium but I wasn't going to ask her for it.

"I will. Thanks." I headed to the elevator and went back up. When I got to my room I headed straight to the shower, spent a good twenty minutes in there, and when I got out, Oscar was already stretched out on the bed. I got my mesh Nike shorts out of my bag, slid them on, and clicked on the TV. I turned off the lamp and scanned the channels. Too emotionally numb to be interested in anything that came up, I just left it on a baseball game with the sound off, got into bed, and closed my eyes.

* * *

I was back on the beach and the ocean had turned black. The wave had swallowed Elyse whole and dragged her out to sea with it.

And it was all my fault.

I'd brought her here and I'd let her run down the beach by herself.

I could go out and swim after her though. She had to be alive. Why would the wave just take her and then kill her?

I set my bare foot in the water and it began to vibrate. Just small little ripples around my foot at first, but then the vibration spread. A second later the water was shaking about ten feet farther along the stretch of beach and then it spread farther than that. I tried to step out of the water but my foot was stuck and as more of the ocean started to shake my foot started to burn.

I desperately tried to get my foot out but it only made it burn hotter, and now the entire ocean was vibrating so fast it'd become a massive black blur. My eyes watered and I frantically pulled at my leg, but I couldn't move it.

I looked out at the ocean and saw that the wave was now coming for me. It stormed over the water like an enraged sea monster and I closed my eyes and waited for it to take me.

Maybe it would take me to Elyse, maybe somewhere different. But I'd made such a mess of things at this point that I deserved whatever I got.

And then the wall of water crashed onto me and dragged me out to sea.

* * *

I felt the blanket slide over my feet and for a second couldn't remember where I was. When it all flooded back into my mind, I turned onto my back and stared at the ceiling as the glow from the TV shifted and flickered over it.

The blanket tugged some more against my legs.

"Don't steal my blanket, Oscar," I said.

He pulled it right off me.

"Damn it, Oscar," I said as I sat up. Oscar sometimes liked to move to the foot of the bed and take the blan—

Oscar was curled up on the other side of the bed.

For a couple of seconds I listened to him softly breathe and stared at the blanket hanging off the end of the bed.

My heart was beating hard.

And then the rest of the blanket slid off of the bed and my heart damn near exploded through my chest.

I leapt out of bed, turned on the lamp, and went to the blanket.

It lay by itself in a heap on the floor.

I took my phone off the nightstand. It was 3:13 a.m.

I went into the bathroom, splashed water on my face, and stared at my bloodshot eyes and unshaven face in the mirror.

"I'm cracking up," I whispered. The stress of Elyse being gone, my blanket falling on the floor by itself, being stranded in some nowhere town where I knew no one. I shut the faucet off and walked out of the bathroom.

I froze the instant my feet hit the carpet.

The closet door was open.

My muscles felt cold and stiff, as if I'd just stepped into a meat locker. I stepped forward and Oscar snorted, sat up, and started growling at the wire hangers and empty space.

I went to the front door—still double locked.

Oscar's low, steady growl was like nothing I'd ever heard from him and I walked towards the closet. When I got there I peeked in to see nothing but a few mothballs on the floor and a sealed deck of playing cards. "Nothing in here, Oscar," I said.

But how the hell could the door open itself and what was making Oscar go into red-alert mode?

The window rattled as a strong wind howled outside. I went up to it and looked out. Most of the storefront lights were off but the street lamps lit up parts of the town in a hazy glow while other sections—particularly the perimeter around the building across the street—were almost totally dark.

Sometimes a lonely town hides things in the shadows.

I rubbed my head. Maybe J.T. *had* known something.

Or—as I had suspected before—maybe I was just flipping out.

Oscar stopped growling, jumped off the bed, and sat down next to me. The corner street lamp and the hotel sign gave off enough light so I could see the outlines of the windows and the heavy door of the building, but it was mostly a big block of darkness. I gazed at it and a flicker of blue light deep in the darkness caught my eye. Oscar lay down next to my feet and I stared at the spot where I thought I'd seen the light.

A little girl in a blue dress floated out of the shadow into the streetlight and my spine chilled and my heart nearly jumped out of my throat.

Her face was a blurry shade of pink and her arms and legs wisps of white light. I couldn't see any other facial features at first, but then a pair of glowing gray eyes seemed to open up like a tiny pair of window shades and she looked right up at me. The girl lifted her arm, pointed at me, and then ran a puffy, glowing finger across her throat.

The back of my neck tightened as she turned around and floated back into the darkness.

I turned away from the window and looked down at Oscar. His face was pressed against his paws but his eyes were wide open. "We're going down there, Oscar."

He stared at me for a long second and then pushed himself to his feet.

I went over to the chair, slid my jeans and t-shirt back, on and went to the door. Oscar sat at the foot of the bed staring at me. "Come on, Oscar," I said as I opened the door. Oscar still sat there and I stepped into the hallway. "Last chance, Oscar."

Oscar got up and slowly padded to the door and into the hallway. I closed the door and headed to the elevator. The lights were on in the lobby but there wasn't anyone behind the desk—which was all the better because I didn't want to explain to anyone why I was going for a walk at nearly four in the morning.

When we stepped into the cool night air, I walked into the barren street and looked over at the building. I didn't believe what I'd seen, but I knew I'd seen it. The building loomed like a dark fortress. It didn't have much charm in the daylight and now it was downright intimidating—taunting even.

The haunted house of Gold Pine.

I didn't believe in ghosts but it wasn't something I'd ever given any serious thought to either.

And how had she known to look up at my room?

Why did she look up at my room?

Oscar let out a sharp bark at the building and his back muscles tensed.

"Quiet, Oscar," I said.

Oscar barked again and started to growl.

I knelt down and rubbed the side of his face. "It's OK, Oscar." But Oscar didn't believe me and neither did I. His growl got deeper and angrier and suddenly he shot towards the building.

Before I could even call out his name he'd disappeared into the shadows.

"Oscar," I called out—not too loudly.

Nothing.

"Oscar, come back," I tried again.

Still nothing. I walked towards the building until I was at the edge of the light. I knew he'd come out. He never ran off. And so I waited.

A minute went by, and then two.

"Oscar," I called again a little louder.

My hands trembled and I turned my cell phone flashlight on, holding it up to the darkness. The white light struggled to penetrate the shadows; it was a solid black wall with barely enough light creeping through to see that Oscar wasn't there.

And then the crying started again.

I did my best to ignore it and began to walk around the building. "Oscar?" I quietly called out. The crying followed me like it did before and as I made my way to the back of the building it got louder and louder. I called out for Oscar again, turned the corner of the building, and frantically waved the phone around. The darkness swallowed up the light like it was deliberately trying to hide Oscar from me, and as I rounded the next corner of the building my heart sank—I wasn't going to find him.

The crying was fainter now, like the ghost girl was being muffled by a sock or something, and I walked back to the street with no idea of what I should do. Should I run around town looking for him? Should I go back into the hotel and sit in the lobby, hoping he'd come scratching at the door soon?

I didn't know.

And so I stood there, wondering how I'd managed to lose the only things I loved in the last twelve hours. My daughter, whom I loved more than anything and the only real reason for me to try to be the best man I could be, was missing because I'd failed to protect her. And my dog, who was my best friend and the only thing I truly trusted, had run off to God knows where or been taken by God knows what.

My throat swelled up and now the tears started to fall.

Another blast of wind shot down the street and hit my cheek like a hard, cold smack. I knew I should go back into the hotel and get some sleep, but I couldn't get my feet to move.

So I just stood there.

Wondering and waiting.

BOOK TWO

I opened my eyes but couldn't get myself out of bed. It felt like a thousand pound weight was sitting on my chest and my muscles were tight and cold. How life had completely gone to hell in the last 24 hours was beyond me, but it had, and now I just wanted to lay here and drift off somewhere far away.

My daughter had vanished, and as if that wasn't enough, my yellow lab, Oscar, had run off into the night. When it rains it pours and this was a typhoon.

But I couldn't just lay here. It wouldn't do any good for me and it sure as hell wouldn't do any good for Elyse or Oscar. I imagined driving in my car with the windows down and Elyse singing along with the radio while Oscar stuck his head out the window, his tongue wagging.

And I felt a small surge of energy.

I was going to find them and it was time to get up.

Rubbing my hands together to generate a little body heat, I pushed myself out of bed, took a shower and got dressed.

Five minutes later I was downstairs in the small hotel breakfast room drinking coffee and eating scrambled eggs and toast. Each forkful of egg felt like it weighed ten pounds and the rye toast felt like I was swallowing cardboard.

But it wasn't the food. The eggs and toast were fine. It was me.

Stress makes your body do some very funny things and right now I could have had the world's most expensive caviar omelet in front of me and I would have wanted to spit it out.

But I had to get something in me and I forced the food down. The last thing I needed was to get so burnt out that I started looking like some kind of scrawny junkie who'd wandered out of the woods into town.

I picked up the coffee and took a sip. The caffeine gave my dark mood a bit of a boost and as I took another drink my phone lit up.

It was Sheriff Eastman.

I picked up the phone and tapped "Accept". "Hello," I said.

"Hello, Mr. Walker?"

"Yes, how are you Sheriff?"

"I'm fine, thank you. I want to give you an update on what's going on."

Updates were for sports and the weather, not 12-year-old daughters, but I kept my attitude to myself. "Okay," I said.

"All right, I'm at the site of your crash right now. There's been no sign of your daughter yet, and in fact, there's no trace of her footprints either. There is however, what appears to be an attempt to cover up an adult-sized track of footprints."

The sheriff paused and I felt like my heart was trying to squirm its way up my throat. "What do you mean?" I asked.

"When we inspected the area around your car, particularly the side of the road covered in dirt before you reach the grass, we saw that dirt had been clumped up in certain spots. When we removed the dirt we discovered what looked like a man's 11 or 12 sized shoe print."

"So somebody took her?" I asked.

"It looks that way," the sheriff responded.

I took a deep breath and let it out. "Okay, so what's next? What can I do?"

"The best thing you can do Mr. Walker is to stay in town and wait for me to call again. Jasper City has been sealed since last night. No one is getting through there without being searched. So if someone has your daughter they're either going to get caught there, or--"

"Or in Gold Pine," I said.

"Correct," he said. "My deputy, Jonathan Colt, is watching over things right now while I'm out here."

My hand had started to tremble but I tried to pick up my coffee again. The cup shook as I lifted it off the table, making little waves off coffee that were about to splash over the rim and I just set it back down.

"So that's where we're at right now," Eastman said. "I'll probably be out here another hour or so and I'll call you as soon as I'm back in Gold Pine. How does that sound?"

I gazed at the basket full of mini cereal boxes on the counter against the smooth yellow wall; Frosted Flakes, Fruit Loops, Lucky Charms - all the sugary cereals that Elyse loves and that Nicole diligently kept her away from.

"Mr. Walker?"

"Yeah, sorry. Okay, that's fine. Just please call me as soon as you're back in town," I said.

"I will, Mr. Walker. Are you okay for now then?"

Okay? What the hell did that mean? My daughter was missing and my dog had vanished into the night. "Yeah, I'm all right," I said.

"Okay, good. I'll be in touch soon."

"Thanks, Sheriff," I said and hung up.

I got up and took what was left of my breakfast to the garbage basket next to the breakfast counter. A half-plate of eggs and a piece of toast would have to be good enough to get me through the morning, because after that chat with Eastman my guilt and nerves weren't going to let my stomach deal with anything more. I tossed the paper plate into the basket and walked out of the room and back into the hallway that led to the front of the hotel. The hallway was lined with black and white photos of the town and I glanced over them as I headed back to the lobby; Ansel Adams-styled shots of the big mountain, panoramic views of the town, even an aerial view of the cemetery. They were lonely, eerie images. There was more to see in them than just a quick glimpse allowed and I was tempted to stop and study them.

But I kept moving - I had to get on with the day.

When I stepped into the lobby, it was a little disconcerting to see Clare, from yesterday gone. There was a thin guy wearing black framed glasses with short black hair neatly parted at the side, running the show now.

He looked up as I entered the lobby. "Good morning, sir," he said as he guided his glasses back up the bridge of his nose.

"Good morning," I said with half a smile. "Do you know if Clare is working today?"

"Yes, she'll be in at 2:00. Is there a message you would like me to give her?"

"No, that's okay. I was just wondering," I said.

"Very good, sir," he said. "My name is Danny if you need any help."

I needed help all right. "Okay, thanks, Danny."

"My pleasure, sir," he said with a nod and went back to whatever he was reading.

Despite my misery, I had to say this was one polite town.

When I got to the entrance I pushed open the door and stepped out into sunlight. The warm rays against my face felt great but, as with other things since Elyse disappeared, it felt bad to feel good. I stepped to the edge of the street and looked over the town. Things were already buzzing and I was treated to the same basic scene that I saw when I arrived yesterday. Women bustling in and out of the shops, a couple of kids circling around on their bikes, and a handful of men reading the newspaper or talking on cell phones.

Of course none of it interested me.

What did interest me was going back down to the cemetery. The sheriff had told me not to leave town, but I didn't think heading over to the residential area was what he meant. Hell, the cemetery was only a quarter of a mile off Main Street at the most, and frankly, I didn't care if he didn't want me to go there anyway. My gut told me the cemetery was a key to finding Oscar and if Sheriff Eastman was going to be in charge of locating my daughter, I'd be damned if I wasn't going to at least work at getting my dog back.

I started to cross the street and stopped. The haunted warehouse. I couldn't believe I'd forgotten about its little role in all of this.

Was the girl watching me right now?

Did she come out during the day?

Even in the sunlight and the busy street I didn't want to walk past it. Somehow the building seemed darker today, like the sun had burned it a darker shade of gray and the damn thing had something unpleasant in store for me when I got too close.

A warm breeze blew from the direction of the warehouse, wrapped around me and slid into my ears. *"Where is sheeeee?"* The back of my neck felt like tiny bugs were dancing on it and I stared at the building. A girl's face, as if traced from a pencil sketch, pressed up against the first side window. The wind then vanished as fast as it had come up on me and the face dissolved. My heart thumped in quick, hard beats but I started walking again. Screw it - the building wanted to push me, I'd push it right back.

I quick-stepped to the sidewalk and kept my eyes focused on the cemetery. My heart thumped against my chest even faster with the anticipation of hearing the girl's cries sink through the glass and into my ears, but she stayed quiet. Right now it was simply an abandoned building. A single eyesore on an otherwise picture perfect small town street.

And the cemetery was straight ahead.

I stepped onto the grass and Nicole's face popped into my head. Just before she died we'd planned on taking a trip to a bunch of ghost towns in the southwest. It was a way to get our marriage going again and she'd been excited. I'd been out of prison for a couple of months and finally she'd been coming around to the idea that I'd been set up. How she could have ever thought I would have embezzled millions of dollars was beyond me but she'd come from a true-blue law-and-order family - her dad had been a marine, a cop, and eventually a prosecuting attorney - and she struggled with the concept that our holy legal system could ever make a mistake.

But Nicole did love me and after my experience she could at least grasp the idea that people in power positions weren't perfect. After that, our marriage had started to get back to the way it had been before those weasels had framed me and we were on our way to being a nice, happy family again.

And then she was gone.

And now Elyse was too.

But I was getting my daughter back. If Sheriff Eastman couldn't do it, I would.

I felt another warm gust as I stepped onto the path. Whereas the warehouse looked darker, the cemetery seemed brighter today. Sunlight blazed against the tombstones, making them look like fiery white rocks. I quickened my pace. I didn't know what, but something was down there. Something connected to the town, something that knew about the warehouse.

Or maybe I was just feeling better because the sun was out.

When I got to the gate, I paused and scratched my chin as I looked over the cemetery - it was the first time in years I'd felt any real stubble. I gazed at the tombstones and then over to the field of grass that stretched beyond.

A set of tracks ran through the gate and into the graveyard. Dog tracks.

They were hard to see, just a faint outline in the bent grass, but a handful of paw prints were indented into the closely cropped blades. I followed the tracks that lined the side of the trail. After about twenty feet, the tracks became frenzied, almost like a crazy dance, moving around in a zig zag sort of pattern.

I looked at the tombstone I was standing in front of. It was Jessica Ray's.

"Oscar!" I called out. "Oscar! Come here boy! Oscar!," I yelled as I turned my head back towards town and my heart froze.

Two hooded figures wearing black cloaks stared at me from about sixty feet away. Neither of them moved a muscle and as much as I tried to see what they looked like, the inside of their hoods were dark cavernous shadows. The one on the right raised his hand and pointed a long finger at me. My legs quivered, but I kept my eyes locked on them.

The sound of wings flapping whooshed through the air behind me and I looked back to see a raven sitting on Jessica's tombstone. I didn't know for sure, but it sure as hell looked like the same bird I saw yesterday. It tilted its head as it stared at me, and then stuck its beak forward like it was pointing at something and let out a booming "caw" that shook my ears like scratchy thunder. I looked back at the field but the cloaked weirdoes were gone and I just stared for a few seconds at the blades of grass bristling in the wind. A car on Main Street honked and I turned back to the raven. He tilted his head and stared at me for a couple of seconds. Then he flew off like he was late to go scare some kids at a Halloween party.

Now that I was seemingly alone again, I looked back down at the dog tracks. There wasn't any trail of them leaving the area. It was just a grassy island of skittishness and then they just vanished. A huge gust of wind whipped across the cemetery and I stumbled sideways, bracing myself with my foot to keep from falling over. It was still nice and sunny out but I guessed that the wind was a sign of rougher weather to come. My gut told me that I'd found everything I was going to for now. I was spooked by those strange cloaked men and it was time to get out of here.

As I walked back up the path towards the town, I remembered my smashed car and jogged the rest of the way back to Main Street. I walked past the shops deciding which one I should go into to ask where the mechanic's place was. Most of them had at least a few customers in them and I didn't feel like getting that close to people yapping about their kids or their boring plans for the day. I looked across the street and the ice cream shop caught my eye. The road was clear and I crossed over, barely noticing the trio of women with shopping bags walking towards me as they whispered to each other.

Did they know who I was? Did they know about Elyse? This was a small town but I didn't think Sheriff Eastman would just let people know about my situation without first telling me - or make it public this soon. I let the women walk past me like I didn't even see them and then went into the ice cream place. A teenage boy with thick red hair in a green University of Oregon t-shirt stood behind the counter reading some kind of computer game magazine. He looked up and smiled as I walked in.

"How you doing today, sir?" he asked.

"I'm all right," I said. "Listen, do you know if there's an auto mechanic's shop nearby?"

"Sure, Big Al's Motor Shop," the kid said with a big grin like it was the thrill of his day to be able to help. "Just make a right out of the shop and then another right at Darb street. You'll see Big Al's almost right away."

"Great, thanks," I said.

"Can I get you anything while you're here? A frosty or something?" he asked.

"No thanks," I said. "Not really an ice cream kind of day for me."

"Yeah, I understand," the kid said shaking his head as he looked back down at the magazine again. "I've worked here for two years and can't stand the stuff anymore."

I nodded, walked to the door and stepped back outside. The next cross street was about a half-block away - I couldn't read the sign yet but I assumed it was Darb Street - and I headed to it. I hadn't paid any attention to what was down there when I'd walked past it the first time, but when I turned the corner I saw a black parking lot in front of a white two-door garage about a hundred feet down. Both doors were up and a red tow truck was parked at the far side of the garage. As I walked down the street, Big Al's Motor Shop appeared in green letters on top of the white, shed-sized office building next to the garage.

There was nothing much else down this way. A little electrical plant was across the street and the road disappeared into the forest about another quarter-mile down - that was it. I crossed the street, and when I reached the garage, saw a guy in jeans wearing an oversized black, Metallica t-shirt kneel down with a wrench to a black Jeep Cherokee. The shirt looked like it could fit a rhino and the big guy locked the wrench against the front hubcap and started to twist like the screws were set in stone.

"Excuse me," I said as I stepped up to the garage entrance.

He stopped and looked up at me with beads of sweat glistening off his forehead.

"Are you Big Al?"

He put the wrench down, picked up a cloth that had been laying on the other side of him and wiped the sweat away. "Yeah, I'm Al. What can I do for ya?"

"My car's wrapped around a tree a few miles out of town and I was told you could rescue it for me."

"Oh yeah, the sheriff mentioned something about that to me. Yeah, I can go get it for you. I've got to finish this job up first though. How's about two hours?"

"Okay," I said. I hated to have to waste the time. Two hours was an eternity with my daughter missing, but what choice did I have? "Is it okay if I head out there with you?"

"Sure, that's no problem. Just meet me back here at one and we'll go get it."

"Okay, thanks," I said.

Al nodded and went back to work with the wrench.

I turned and started walking back to Main Street. I didn't want to aggravate the sheriff but I was getting antsy and I wanted to get back to where I'd lost Elyse. Maybe something would ring a bell or I'd spot something that would help me get back to her.

I was feeling desperate.

I got back to Main Street and for the next couple of hours roamed around. I grabbed a quick lunch at a soup and sandwich shop called The Lunch Box and kept my eyes peeled for Oscar.

At about ten to one I headed back to Big Al's. He was leaning against his truck eating a sub sandwich and nodded as

I walked up to him. "Just give me a second," he said between bites. The sub of thick toasted bread looked like it was stuffed with every lunch meat on Earth, with what looked like Italian dressing dripping down the side and onto the ground. Big Al gobbled the last of it up. "Damn things," he said as he scrunched up the wrapping and took a swig of Coke. "I used to eat them five days a week, now I've cut it to three. Trying to drop twenty pounds. You look pretty lean, you work out?"

"Yeah, a little," I said scratching the back of my tightening neck. "Look, my car is wrapped around a tree in the middle of nowhere and I really want to get it back here as quickly as possible."

Al nodded and walked over to the trash can in front of his shop. He tossed the wrapper in and headed back to me. He took another drink of Coke and pointed at the passenger side. "Hop in. We'll go get your car."

I grabbed the handle, pressed the thick silver button, the door popped open and I climbed in. Big Al hauled himself into the truck and slammed the door. Reaching into his pocket, he pulled out a gold key ring that had a silver skull with black eyes and three bronze keys hanging from it. Al slipped one of the keys in the ignition, turned it, and the engine rumbled. "And we're off," he said as he hit the gas and drove out of the parking lot. We drove down Second Street and then made a left onto Main. A minute later we were rolling past the thick green forests towards my wreck.

"So what happened to ya out here?"

I told him about swerving to miss the deer and slamming into the tree and Al nodded. "Yeah, happens almost every year out here. You'd think the damn things would learn by now to look before they run across."

I nodded and watched as the trees went by in a green blur. It suddenly occurred to me that Sheriff Eastman could still be out here, but it seemed unlikely. How long could he spend at the crash site? It'd been a little over three hours since I'd heard from him this morning and I was tempted to call him but held off. I wasn't supposed to be out here anyway and there was no reason he wouldn't have called me already if he had something to tell me.

The truck veered left and I could see my smashed car about a hundred feet away.

"Damn," Big Al said as we got closer. "You really did do a number on this thing, didn't ya?"

I didn't say anything and a second later we pulled up alongside my car.

"Phew, I'll tell you right now, son," he said looking out the open window at my car, "this is going to cost a pretty penny to fix. You got insurance?"

"Yeah. The deductible is about a grand."

"Shoot, you don't have to worry about that. We're going clear past that. Hell, you might want to just sell it to me and get yourself a new car."

"No," I said snapping off my seatbelt. "Just fix it."

"Whatever you want, boss," he said as he opened the door and jumped out of the truck, his work boots hitting the road with a thud that sounded like a tiny earthquake tremor.

I got out of the truck too and stared down the road. It was lonely out here. Like a big green haunted house - and Elyse could be anywhere in it. I walked over to the car while Big Al fidgeted with the hook on the back of his truck.

"Need any help, Al?" I asked as I looked over my wrecked car. It did appear to be in the same exact condition I'd left it in yesterday. I had figured the hubcaps would be gone or something, but at least the two on this side were still here.

"I'm all right," he said. "Just takes a second to unhook this damn thing sometimes."

I nodded, walked to the other side of the car and my gut went hollow while my chest turned so cold it was like a big block of ice. Sheriff Eastman sat on the grass with his back propped up against the car and a bullet hole in the side of his head. A stream of dried blood oozed down his face. My legs were as stiff as the Tin Man's but I managed to take a couple of steps towards the sheriff. His eyes were wide open and his badge had been shoved in his mouth.

Big Al started to whistle while he worked and I just stared at the dead law man.

"We've got a problem here, Al," I said swallowing hard.

"The sheriff is sitting here, dead."

Big Al scrambled around the car. "Well, I'll be damned. Poor bastard."

"Yeah," I said, rubbing my head. There wasn't a doubt in my mind that who'd ever done this was the one who'd taken Elyse.

"That takes some son-of-a-bitch to shoot down a town sheriff like this," Big Al said in a faraway voice. "Eastman was a great guy, really took care of the town. And some psycho does this to him. I've got half a mind to go back to the shop and get my shotgun to hunt this sucker down."

"Yeah, Eastman seemed like a real decent guy," I said in a very controlled voice, barely able to keep myself from screaming at the sky as loud as I could. This nightmare had been bad enough, now the guy I was counting on to make everything better was leaning against my smashed car with his brains blown out.

"Deputy Colt is going to be pretty shaken up over this. He's been with Sheriff Eastman for years. The sheriff actually recruited Colt to come work for him," Big Al said. "Life sure has a sick way of working."

The thick streak of dark purple blood looked like it had been dry for a while. How long after he'd talked to him had this happened? An hour? Less? My stomach felt like it had a black hole swirling inside of it and my mind raced. It was like my life had been nothing but a house of cards that had just been kicked over.

"Listen Al, I'm going to tell you something," I said.

"Yeah?" the big man asked.

"Sheriff Eastman was out here investigating my missing daughter. She'd been with me when we crashed yesterday and when I woke up she was gone."

Al took a deep breath and let it out. He said nothing for a long second and then took a couple of steps closer to the sheriff's corpse and put his hands on his hips. "Well, guess we better call it in to Deputy Colt. Hopefully we can catch him in the office."

"What should we do about the car?" I asked.

"Let's just leave it here right now. Colt won't want the scene messed with until he can check it out. I'll bring the car in after he's done."

I nodded and said nothing.

What the hell was there to say?

Daughter gone, dog gone, sheriff murdered.

I followed Al back to the truck and climbed in. Al turned the key and we rumbled off.

"The sheriff really was a good man," he said as his hands trembled slightly against the steering wheel. "I don't know, whole damn world's gone crazy. You'll find your daughter though. I've got a gut feeling about these things and you'll find her."

"Thanks," I said quietly. It was like a repeat of a bad dream. It was as if yesterday and today had blended into each other with the little twist that I now got to go tell the Gold Pine deputy that his boss had been murdered.

Big Al took out his phone, hit a couple of buttons and set it to his ear. A few seconds went by and he hung the phone up. "Got Colt's voicemail. We'll just tell him when we see him," he said as he slid the phone back into his pocket

We drove in silence for the next few minutes and when we got back into Gold Pine, Big Al dropped me off in front of the sheriff's office. Al was going to park the truck and come back over after that. I walked up the steps to the office and then looked back out at the town. It was a little quieter today and everyone seemed like they were moving a little slower - or maybe my brain was just slowing down. I thought about the neck rubs Nicole used to give me after one of my twelve hour days at the office. We'd put on a movie and a lot of times Elyse would come wandering into our room with Oscar and sit down on the floor. Eventually we'd all fall asleep and when I got up in the morning Elyse would be curled up with Oscar at the edge of the bed.

Somebody told me once that life is fluid.

Nobody said it was radioactive though.

I pushed the door open and walked in.

A fit guy who looked like he spent a lot of time in the sun and ran Iron Man triathlons stood at the desk where Lori, the secretary had been working yesterday. He was reading something on the computer and looked up at me with wide eyes. "Can I help you?" he asked.

"Yeah, are you by any chance, Deputy Colt?" I asked.

"Yes, I am," he said. "Do you need some help?"

"I do," I said.

When I told the deputy about the sheriff, his jaw dropped and his tan face turned pale. "Oh, man," he said looking down and rubbing his chin. "I told him to let me go out there with him." Deputy Colt sighed and I could see his hand tremble a bit. "All right, I'm going to get out there and have the body taken care of and Big Al can bring your car back to his shop. We need to keep this quiet though. This is a small, remote town and if people find out that Sheriff Eastman has been murdered before we have any kind of handle on things, it'll make it that much tougher to get to the bottom of this. You understand Mr. Walker?"

"Yeah, I do," I said sliding my hands into the side pockets of my jeans.

"Okay, good. And one other thing, please, do not leave town again until you hear from me, okay? We don't know what we're dealing with yet but I'll at least know how to find you."

"All right," I said. I thought about telling Colt about the ghostly girl outside the warehouse last night, but decided against it. Who knew what he might have known - or not known - about her and the last thing I needed was him thinking I had a screw loose. "You've got my number, deputy?"

"Yes, I do," he said checking his phone.

"Okay, thanks." I walked out of the office.

So now Deputy Colt was on the case. My muscles had
started to feel weak and chilled from the stress and my
stomach growled. It'd been almost five hours since I'd had
my breakfast and I figured I should get something in me. I
went across the street, bought myself an 8 inch meatball sub
and a Coke and went back outside. For the next ten minutes
I wandered around eating my sub and peering into store
windows without paying any attention to what I was looking
at. When I came up to a bookstore I hadn't noticed before, I
threw the last third of my sandwich and half-filled Coke in the
trash can at the side of the curb and went inside.

Five levels of bookshelves lined the walls of the store
called Carly's Books. An older woman who looked like she
was in her upper-fifties, with tightly pulled back blond hair
had a stack of books in her hands and was looking over the
third shelf on the right wall. She set one of the books on the
shelf and looked over at me and smiled. "Taking a break from
the sunshine, sweetie?" she asked.

"Yeah, guess so," I said as I walked towards the sand-
colored wooden shelves that took up the middle of the space.
They were a good ten feet high and ran almost the full length
of the shop. It was the first time I actually felt secure in this
town, as if all the books were protecting me from the nasty
reality of the outside. As I traced my index finger along the
hardcover titles, I came to a book called *Ten Strange Towns
of the West*. I slid the book off the shelf and thumbed through
it. It was a little over 300 pages and there were a lot of pencil

sketched drawings of the various towns. I turned to the front and looked over the table of contents.

I jumped to chapter four.

The first few pages were not exactly setting the paper on fire as I skimmed over them. Town founded in 1923, starting in the 1950s developed a reputation as a quiet resort town, in the 60s and 70s became more of a residential small town, 1980s and 1990s underwent a spark of population growth and a resurgence in vacationers seeking an under-the-radar place for a vacation home or rental.

In 2004 was the first recorded murder in Gold Pine.

In 2007 there was another.

And the third was in 2013. It was of a twelve year old girl. Jessica Ray.

I shut the book and went up to the register where the woman was now happily gazing out the store window.

"Find everything okay, dear?" she asked as I set the book down on the counter.

"Yeah, I did."

She smiled at me like I was an eight year old who'd just announced how much he loved to read, and then she scanned the book. "$17.95," she said.

I gave her a twenty. "Keep the change," I said and hurried out before she could finish saying "have a nice day." Back outside, I held my new purchase tightly under my arm and started to walk back to the hotel. The entire day had felt like I'd been grasping at invisible straws. It seemed as if this book could give me some insight into what the hell was going on in this town.

When I got back to the hotel, Clare was behind the desk and she beamed at me when I walked in. "How are you, Mr. Walker?"

"I'm okay, Clare. Thanks." I could see she wanted to ask about Elyse but was smart enough to hold back. "Oh, one thing, Clare. My dog, Oscar ran off last night. You haven't seen him have you?"

"Oh, no. I'm sorry, Mr. Walker. I haven't, but I'll keep my eyes open for him."

"Thanks, Clare. I'd appreciate that. I'm just going to go up to my room for a second and then I'm going back out."

"Okay, Mr. Walker," she said.

I took the elevator, went to my room and set the book on the bed. This was like being trapped in a horrific *Twin Peaks* episode and I badly wanted to read more, but I needed to get back outside to search for Oscar. I then went back to the lobby and moved through it like I was late for a meeting - I figured me and Clare could use a break from the niceties. The sky was still a clear blue, but wisps of white cloud now floated overhead. Oscar hated the rain and I hoped it would at least stay dry for him.

But rain or shine, I was finding my dog.

I spent the next two hours wandering the town and the residential areas trying to find any other trace of Oscar, but I had no luck. There were the tracks at the tombstone and that was it. It was now almost four thirty and as I made my way up Main Street for the fourth or fifth time I watched a group of five girls around the age of eleven or twelve, in pink, green, and blue dresses giggling in front of the bookstore I'd be in before. One of them held her phone out and the rest of them bunched up next to her posing like little drama queens.

The rest of them except one.

She didn't laugh, she didn't smile, and her face was a fuzzy cloud, like an eraser had rubbed out her eyes, nose, and mouth.

And as she stepped away from the group and walked over to the curb, she stood straight as an arrow with her diffuse hand, pointing her finger at me. Not a single girl seemed to notice or care.

My heart started cranking away again and I stopped walking. The ghost girl took a crooked step into the street and her body jerked like it had gotten an electric shock. I stared as she took yet another jagged step and a BMW drove right through her. The rest of the town now barely seemed to exist, as if it had stretched itself out and the buildings and murmur of people were very far away.

And she kept coming.

Her elbows and knees blurring with each erratic step as she stared at me with eyes dull, dark eyes.

I wanted to run away but my eyes locked into the grayness like a hypnotic fog and my body went numb.

And she kept walking towards me. Her arms now thrashing in the air like she was having a seizure.

Another step and then another. I couldn't hear anything else now but the wind. She stepped on the sidewalk and her arm and hand stretched towards my face as if made from elastic. All of a sudden I could hear and feel the young girl's shrieking cries digging deep into my ears.

"Ryan!" a woman's voice called out, breaking through the noise.

I managed to turn my head and saw Tara, the woman I'd met last night, coming out of the ice cream shop. My entire body had broken into a cold sweat and my knees trembled. I looked back in front of me. The girl was gone and everything was quiet.

"Ryan, how are you? Have you found out anything? " Tara asked walking up to me

Christ, I found something all right. "No, not much yet," I said as my body slowly warmed again.

"How's Sheriff Eastman doing though? Has he been in touch?"

I could barely put together a coherent thought but I did my best to settle down and push the ghostly girl out of my mind and managed to nod. I thought about just telling Tara about Eastman, but I didn't. If Colt wanted me to keep quiet about the sheriff then I was going to. "Yeah, a little," I said watching an old Dodge Ram drive by so I wouldn't have to make eye contact. "We talked this morning."

Tara nodded and didn't push it anymore. Smart people know when to stop asking questions. Her eyes gazed past me and I looked in the same direction to see a wiry blond guy watching us from about a block away. It was the same guy who had been sitting by us at O'Mally's last night. He wore khakis again and his hands were in the pockets of his thin, waist-length leather jacket. An ex-boyfriend? An odd client? He pulled his left hand out of his pocket, checked his watch and walked off.

I ran my hands through my hair and then over my face. Where in the hell was I?

Tara's cheeks were a little tight and she sighed. "Look, Ryan. Please call me tonight, I might be able to help you find your daughter."

"Really? " I asked.

She looked back to where the man had been and nodded. "Yeah, I've got to go now though. You'll call me, right?"

"Yes, absolutely."

"Good." Tara hurried off and I watched her disappear around the next corner.

What the hell kind of info would she have about my daughter? How would she have it? I folded my arms, looked down at the sidewalk and shook my head. I felt like I was a cat chasing a string.

My phone rang and I answered it. "Hello?"

"Yeah, Mr. Walker, it's Al, the mechanic."

"Hey, Al. What's happening?"

"I got your car in my shop and I'll be working on it tomorrow. Do you need a loaner or anything?"

Man, that was tempting. I could get back out there and start searching for Elyse on my own. Hell, it wasn't like I could do worse than Eastman. But I was going to hold off for now. I wasn't law enforcement or any kind of detective and I could only assume the deputy knew what he was doing. "I'm okay right now, but maybe in the next day or so," I said. "How long do you think it'll take to get the car up and running again?"

"Hard to say exactly. Depends if I can salvage the engine or not. I'm also going to have to order some of the parts you need to get her in shape again. I'll put a rush on the order so right now I'd say 3-4 days."

Not awful. "Okay," I said. "Do you need anything else from me, right now?"

"No, I'm all set. Just one thing, Mr. Walker..."

"What's that?" I asked.

"You're staying at the Mountain View, right?"

"Yes, I am."

"You happen to see anything strange while you're over there?"

I swallowed as I thought about an answer. Al seemed like an all right guy but I didn't know him from the man on the moon. "Strange how?" I asked.

"Eh, forget it. Sometimes I just hear things around town. Just give me a call if you need anything, okay?"

"I'll do that, Al. Thanks." He hung up and I slid my phone into my pocket.

Strange things. Understatement of the millennium.

It was now almost six o'clock and I decided to head back to the hotel to try and get a bit of rest. I knew I should probably eat something but I wasn't hungry and I started walking towards Mountain View. Dinner had always been a fun thing with Nicole and Elyse. Elyse loved to cook and Nicole loved being her little helper. Salads had been Elyse's big thing and Nicole would let her come up with all kinds of crazy stuff that usually somehow ended up being pretty good; avocado mixed with cold strips of steak, oranges, apples, and turkey slices, sardines sprinkled with Havarti cheese - she'd been like a little mad-scientist chef with Nicole making sure she didn't put anything together that would turn our stomachs upside down.

When I got back to the hotel, Clare was standing behind the desk reading a magazine. She smiled and waved when I walked in and I did my best to return the favor, but with my state of mind it felt like my smile came out like a deformed smirk. Thankfully, the elevator door was already open and I walked in and went up to my floor.

Once I was back in my room, I took the book off the bed and sat down in the chair by the window. I opened it to the Gold Pine chapter and continued reading.

The first two deaths were what you would call more run-of-the-mill killings. A 37 year old man named Jonah Webb was shot by Derek Cole, a drunk member of a biker gang called the Vampires. And Derek, along with the rest of the gang, had various reported criminal ties. The night of the murder, poor Jonah had been involved in a parking dispute with Derek, who just spent the past couple of hours getting lit up on vodka. Things had gotten very heated very fast and Derek shot Jonah dead on the spot. He was arrested the next day and was currently serving life in prison.

The second death involved the stabbing of a 17 year old boy by a 32 year old man named Jason Barris who had simply wandered into town. No one knew how he got to Gold Pine and no motive was ever released, but medical testimony had shown that Barris had suffered from severe schizophrenia and had spent the prior nine years in and out of the Oregon State Mental Health Clinic. Barris was currently serving thirty years in a maximum security psychiatric institution.

And then there was number three.

The details surrounding Jessica's death were sparse, but she was the reason Gold Pine had made it into the book. She'd lived her whole life in Gold Pine and on her twelfth birthday had gone missing. Three days later her body had been found in a warehouse that stood at the far end of the town's Main

Street. Cuts in bizarre patterns were found over her body, with each wrist being slit. She had been buried the next day in the cemetery just outside of town and a week later the first of what would be numerous sightings was reported of a girl wandering around outside the warehouse at night. In just over three months, seven sightings were reported and two weeks later the warehouse had been sold. After that the sightings had ceased and the building had remained unused and dormant.

I closed the book, stood up, and looked out the window. Sunset was happening and once again the lowering sun's orange light had crept over the town in a fiery glow. The warehouse stayed dark though, like it was immune to the light and was sending a message - a message to me.

Bad things happen here.

The day suddenly started to catch up with me and my eyelids got heavy. I didn't want to sleep but my body felt like it had just finished a double marathon and I just needed to lie down for a while. I crawled on to the bed and lay down on my back. Maybe Deputy Colt would call while I napped. I'd wake up and he'd have a voicemail saying he'd found Elyse and Oscar playing happily with each other just outside of town and they were both at the police station now ready for me to pick them up.

Maybe that would happen.

I felt my mouth turn upwards in a small smile as I drifted off to sleep.

* * *

My eyes popped open when I heard Oscar howling. Had I dreamt it? I didn't think so. Other than the gold glow flowing into the room from the hotel sign, the room was completely dark. I lay there waiting and my heart started to pound when I heard the howl again.

That was Oscar.

I jumped up and hurried out of the room. A minute later I was downstairs cutting through the empty lobby and a second later I was outside in the street. Oscar's howl pierced the night sky and I looked around frantically. "Oscar!" I called out down the street.

I looked back at the warehouse and saw Jessica Ray watching me, standing at the edge of the darkness in the glow of the street lamp. She grinned and her round gray eyes gleamed under the street light. My legs tightened as Jessica lifted her pink, shimmering hand in the air and waved at me. I tried to step back towards the hotel but my legs were paralyzed and I couldn't move. Jessica shook her head at me and her eyes turned black as oil while her grin bent downwards into an angry jack-o-lantern-like frown.

Oscar howled again and this time it seemed to come from straight ahead, beyond the town.

I looked outwards. A purple glow in the cemetery started to blaze like a beacon. An adrenaline rush overrode my paralysis and I ran across the street, managing to turn on the phone's flashlight just as I got to the other side. I found the path with the light and began to quickly walk towards the cemetery, shooting a glance back to see nothing but the dark warehouse and the quiet glow of the Main Street lights.

I hurried down the path, past the side streets dimly lit by flickering street lamps and the late night lights of a couple of houses. I watched as the glow pulsed and throbbed like a steady heartbeat and my hands shook with excitement the closer I got. Another howl came straight out of the cemetery and I walked as fast as I could - not wanting to run because I didn't want to trip in the dark and sprain my ankle or land on my face - which wouldn't do me any good. A few seconds later I reached the cemetery gate and went through. The purple light around Jessica's Ray's tombstone was so strong and so thick that I couldn't even see the stone itself. I walked towards it and shut my phone flashlight off. I called out to Oscar. I didn't see him but I knew he was here. I called his name again and he howled so loud that it almost seemed to shake the ground. But Oscar still didn't appear. He had to know it was me though. He had to know I was here.

When I reached the tombstone I stood in front of it and snapped a picture of it.

"Oscar," I called out again more quietly. "Come here, Oscar. I'm here boy."

A cold wind whipped across the cemetery and the glow vanished like a big purple flame being blown out. It was now almost pitch black and my hands shivered as I fumbled with the phone trying to turn the flashlight back on. When I finally tapped the little flashlight icon, the white beam shot onto the path and I lifted it and shined it on Jessica's tombstone.

A rusty key lay on top of the stone.

I stepped up to Jessica's tombstone and picked it up. It was a bit bigger than your normal key, maybe like something you'd use to open a heavy padlock and I slid it into my jean pocket. I began to scan the cemetery with the flashlight. "Oscar," I said quietly as the light glowed against the various tombstones.

"Oscar's not coming," said a sad voice that sounded like it had come from deep inside a metal funnel. My hands shook so hard that the light flickered spastically over the stones in the row behind Jessica's, just like an angry strobe light. I grabbed my forearm with my other hand and managed to get the light somewhat under control. I then guided the light in the direction of the voices and the beam lit up two bulky figures in black cloaks standing about fifteen feet away from me in the next row. Their hoods were up and their sleeves hung past their hands. One of them took a step towards me.

"And you're not going anywhere, Ryan."

BOOK THREE

I woke up with the side of my face pressed against cold concrete. My head was throbbing and my mind was blank. All I knew was the sensation of the frigid, hard floor and I badly needed five or six Advil. After a few seconds, the cobwebs cleared and it all came flooding back. My daughter had vanished, my dog was gone, that tombstone glowing like bright purple fire had lured me to the cemetery just outside Gold Pine. It was then those two freaks in dark cloaks came after me. The last thing I remember before everything went dark was when one of them had screamed in some kind of weird, eastern European sounding language.

And now I was here.

Wherever that was.

I opened my eyes to see a smooth, gray floor and a set of concrete stairs about twenty feet away. White light lit the room and I turned my head upwards to see half a dozen fluorescent glass tubes attached to the ceiling. It was just like an interrogation scene from a 1950s movie and I had no intention of sticking around to meet its creator. I tried to move my arms to push myself up off the floor, but my wrists pressed into thin, tightly wound rope. In my struggle I became aware that my ankles were bound in the same way. I was being held against my will.

Gazing at the stairs, I tried to think constructively. How would I get out of this? Outside of developing some sort of super power, the situation seemed hopeless. I shut my eyes, took a deep breath and let it out. I'd survived a stint in prison only to have my wife murdered, my daughter disappear, and for an extra pinch of salt in the wound, my dog had run off into the night. And if it all that wasn't bad enough, I was now trapped in some kind of bunker basement by God knows who, getting ready to do God knows what.

I might not have been in the seventh circle of hell, but I felt like I was pretty close.

My eyes snapped back open to what sounded like a casket creaking open coming from the top of the stairs. I saw in the doorway the thin, silhouette of a man standing in front of a yellow-walled hall. As he came down a few steps, the silhouette gathered form to became a thin guy with short blonde hair wearing tight, faded jeans and a black t-shirt. Was the man from O'Malleys' I had watching me and Tara talk on the sidewalk the yesterday?

I did my best to loosen the rope by sliding my wrists under the tight rope, but the heat of the twine burned into my skin and I quickly gave up. Blondie approached me. He crouched down, and slid out a gun that had been tucked into the back of his jeans. He pointed it at my face and tilted his head as his lips curled upward into a wry smile. "Have a nice nap, Mr. Walker?"

"I've had better," I said.

"Hmm," he said nodding as he looked me over. "I'm sure you have. Unfortunately it's not five stars here – or even

Mountainside Hotel for that matter – but we have bigger things on our minds, so you'll have to cut us some slack."

I didn't say anything. I was no James Bond and staring into the barrel of a gun seemed to make smart comebacks a risky proposition.

"Now look Ryan, I want you to listen to me very carefully. Your daughter is extremely important to us, and unfortunately, you're not part of the equation. On the other hand, we can't have you snooping around town looking for her either." Blondie pushed the gun against my forehead and the cold, hard muzzle pressed into my skin. "Now, I'd like to kill you, but that would make things much more complicated for us, so I'm going to make you a first-time last-time offer. You have until sundown to get out of Gold Pine. If you do so, your daughter will live. If not, she will die. If we catch you speaking to law enforcement, she will die. If we see you wandering around the cemetery again, she will die. Do you understand?"

"Where is she," I asked.

He opened a bottle, held a rag over it and turned it upside down. Somehow I knew what was coming. He set the bottle down "Sorry, Ryan. No questions," he said as he pressed the cloth over my face.

When I returned to consciousness I was lying on my back staring at the bright blue sky. Confusion smothered my mind like a thick gray fog and it took almost ten seconds before I felt the sharp blades of grass poking into my back and arms. As the mental haze started to clear, I remembered the basement and that blonde bastard telling me to get out of town or he'd kill Elyse.

But, of course, I wasn't going anywhere. How could I?

My head still ached but my arms and legs were at least free now. I turned over and pushed myself to my feet. I could see the tombstones of the cemetery beaming brightly under the golden rays of the high-noon sun. My body was tight, tired and ached all over. I stretched my arms out and then, with the pressure of my palms on my lower back flexed my back muscles as I turned towards the midday bustle of town. My immediate plan was to get back to the hotel and regroup. If nothing else, and as much as I could believe him, Blondie had given me reason to think that Elyse hadn't been harmed yet. I was clinging to the hope that I could get her back if I worked quickly.

I rubbed my arms for a good half minute to warm my stiff muscles. I then walked with quick, big steps to the path that ran from the cemetery to town.

The sounds of women talking and laughing carried out of Gold Pine like some sort of afternoon soundtrack set on repeat, and I wanted to press my hands over my ears. The more I learned about this place, the more the town's happiness seemed forced. Not in a deliberately manufactured fake way, but it felt compensatory. It was as if the dark side of Gold Pine was a nagging voice in the back of everyone's minds and they were badly trying to drown it out with an overlying sense of good humor.

I could see the usual midday crowd strolling from store to store and I crossed the street and headed back to the hotel. Try as I might I couldn't keep my head turned away from the warehouse. My eyes drifted to it like a radar programmed to spot trouble and I saw that the brick walls were now black and the windows were tinted.

Other than the hotel, there wasn't much going on at this end of the street. But at least a few people hanging around the center part of town had to notice the damn place changing colors. My best guess was that the warehouse was like the weird, crazy uncle in an otherwise nice family; you don't talk about him and you pretend he doesn't exist. Hell, if I lived here I'd probably act like I didn't know about the place either.

I tore my eyes from the warehouse, keeping them locked on the mountain until I reached the hotel, swung open the door and went in. Clare smiled but didn't say anything. I was sure I looked a sight so maybe she didn't want to bother me with questions. I probably looked like something out of a zombie movie right now. Either way, I was grateful not to have to deal with the small-talk and I headed straight for the open elevator door. Two minutes later I was back in my room and I went into the bathroom to strip off my clothes and take a quick shower. Standing under the water, just the sound of the warm spray helped my tight neck muscles to relax and my headache to fade some more. Stepping into the shower, I spent the next ten minutes motionless under the steady stream of hot water, waiting for the rest of my headache to float away. Somewhere inside me was a glimmer of hope that somehow everything would be all right.

When I was done, I dried off and walked back into the room. I went over to the window and my mouth dropped open. A light gray smoke swirled over the entire roof of the warehouse in a way that made it look like some kind of spiraling galaxy. As I gawked at the insanity of it, a girl's blurred face emerged from the smoke like a face bobbing out of a dark ocean. And then just as quickly, it sank back into it.

I rubbed my eyes and when I looked at the roof again it was perfectly dry and flat.

Terrific, I'm losing my mind. What do I do now?

Thoughts of Tara filled my mind.

I went over to the dresser, grabbed my phone, found her name tapped her number and held my breath. A clicking sound came after the third ring and my heart jumped.

"Hello?" Tara said in her alluring, raspy voice that somehow sounded even better on the phone than in person.

"Hi, Tara. It's Ryan. Ryan Walker."

"Ryan, I'm so glad you called. I was worried when I didn't hear from you last night. Are you okay?" she asked.

"Yeah. Although 'okay' is an extremely relative term."

"Listen, I need to see you. But I think it's too dangerous to meet you in town. There's a hidden trail north of town called Angel Eye. It's about a ten minute walk from

Main Street. Take Samson Road which is just across the street from the hotel. You'll come to a couple of very tall, sharp-edged boulders. When you get to the boulders you'll see the trailhead. I'll be waiting for you in an hour, a half-mile down the trail."

Tara hung up and I looked back out the window. The roof of the warehouse still looked normal but my mind spiraled with questions. How the hell had my life come to this? I'd had a family, a dog and a career.

And now I was stuck in a Twilight Zone nightmare where I was being harassed by ghost girls and seeing warehouse roofs smothered with eerie smoke.

But there was no point in moping or questioning the state of my mental health right now. I slid the phone into my pocket and started to head out of the room. I caught a glimpse of myself in the mirror above the dresser, stopped, and stared. My face had thinned, my arms and chest looked like they belonged on an underfed marathon runner, and I had black marks under my eyes. Christ, they should just stick me on the 'Come To Gold Pine' brochure. I wasn't hungry but my diminishing physical state reminded me that I should get something to eat before I headed out to meet Tara. Outside, people were everywhere and Mustangs and 'Vettes revved their engines as they rolled down the street, but everything sounded muted, like the town's volume had been turned way down.

Nicole had been heavy into psychology and yoga and she'd talked a lot about how the mind can play funny tricks on your body when it's under duress – apparently this was one of those times. Still, I couldn't waste time worrying about my precious mind/body connection. I just needed some energy and then I would go meet Tara. I looked down the street, saw a blue sign next to the sub place I'd been to yesterday. I kept my head down to avoid making eye contact with anyone as I made my way to *Jacob's Deli*. A little bell on a string rang out as I pulled opened the glass door. A thin, bald man somewhere in his mid-fifties drying a glass with a white rag looked up and smiled. "How you doing today, son?"

"You wouldn't believe me if I told you," I said.

"Eh, I might," he said with a chuckle. "What can I get you?"

I ordered a pastrami and Coke and the guy nodded and went into the kitchen to the side of the counter. Five minutes later I had the sandwich and five minutes after that I'd finished it and was back outside. The sky had darkened to a cloudless deep blue but the sun was still nice and bright. A curvy, thirty-something year old woman in black Nike shorts and a purple body-fit tank top jogged past me. Her bouncing black ponytail reminded me of how Nicole used to tie her hair back for her morning runs. I watched as she ran past a couple of guys in expensive-looking beige suits who nodded at her before turning their heads to watch as she ran past them into the distance. Turning my gaze towards Darb Road, I wondered for a second if Big Al had begun work on my car yet - not that it mattered to me at this point. Right now, I didn't care what happened to the old Buick. I just had to find out what Tara had for me and I jogged across the street and headed back towards the hotel.

Until Tara had mentioned it, I'd never noticed a name of the cross street between Mountain View and the vacant shop on the opposite corner, and when I came up to it I could see why. There was no street sign. Turning, I looked down the road. "Samson" was painted in thick red letters on the curb about thirty feet away.

This f'ing town.

I shrugged and started walking down the street, which like Darb Road yesterday, disappeared into the woods about fifty yards away. An empty parking lot sat behind the vacant shop and beyond that a strip of grass stretched along the road. Just past the "Samson" sign, a sand-covered pavement with fist sized rocks scattered over it, spread out from the back of the hotel almost like a patch of desert moonscape. And after that it was just a field of grass that led up to the woods.

I picked up the pace and a couple of minutes later stepped under the shade of the forest's massive trees. The sun trickled through the leaves and branches onto the road and I looked back to see the empty street leading back to the town. I dearly hoped no one had watched me come down here. For whatever it was worth, my gut told me I hadn't been. Blondie hadn't struck me as someone who'd be spending the entire day watching me and he had his own plans to take care of anyway – whatever those were. Either way, it didn't matter. Tara was my only hope of getting Elyse back and I had no choice but to head down there.

As I walked along the side of the road, just a foot or so from the grass, a chorus of birds hidden in the trees started to sing. A cool breeze blew at me ruffling the leaves and causing the grass to sway and goosebumps popped up on my forearms. The woods, this town, everything seemed eerie, but maybe if I'd been here on a nice little vacation instead of searching for my abducted daughter, it would feel different. Since losing Elyse, my enjoyment sensors had been shut off. My life as I knew it had just become this sort of distant slide show of strangely unattainable images. It all felt unnatural and weirdly "off".

Of course, I didn't believe for a second that the strange blond man and his partner weren't going to hurt Elyse if I left town. They wanted me gone for obvious reasons, but I knew damn well it had nothing to do with how they would treat Elyse. They were going to do what they were going to do, and it was up to me to stop it. Which begged the question: what in the hell were they up to?

I shuddered and blocked out the scary answers my imagination came up with.

The road veered left and I saw, in a clearing about thirty feet away and in front of the woods, two rocks as tall as lampposts with sharp, pointed edges. Rounding the bend, I peered through the oval-shaped space that separated the giant boulders at a trail of hard-packed dirt that stretched deep into the woods. I couldn't see Tara yet, but she'd said she'd be farther down the trail and I hoped to hell she was already here. I stepped off the road and headed towards the rocks. I took out my phone and my heart jumped when I saw that Deputy Colt had called and left a voicemail. Blondie had told me not to talk to the law and I believed he was quite serious. But this would just be checking my phone and how the hell would he know anyway? I had to force myself to put those thoughts aside, so I tapped the screen and put the phone to my ear.

"Hello, Mr. Walker, this is Deputy Colt. I wanted to let you know that at this point I don't have any new information as to the whereabouts of your daughter, but I'm pursing the matter vigilantly and will update you as soon as I discover anything. Please feel free to call me if you have any questions."

The message ended as I side-stepped through the opening and walked onto the trailhead. This was as far as I went with Colt. He hadn't come up with anything and I didn't have any questions. Besides, Sheriff Eastman had already met his own nasty fate and I could only assume it was Blondie and his thick-necked friend who'd delivered it to him. As far as I was concerned – and aside from whatever help Tara could give me - I was on my own from here.

I deleted the message and began to walk down the trail. The four or five foot wide path ran straight for about a hundred yards before curving to the right and disappearing behind the dark green forest. Looking up, I felt a little bit of relief to the somewhat claustrophobic feeling the trail was giving me as I gazed over the thick sliver of blue sky visible between the trees. A sunbeam hit the trail about twenty feet away. My skin tightened up at the sudden realization of just how silent the trail was. The bright chirping of the birds had faded so much that it was now like listening to a radio on the other side of a thick wall, and other than the occasional quick crunching sound of a squirrel scrambling between the trees, there was next to no ambient noise. Rubbing my hands together, I looked back up at the sky and then gazed ahead as I started to round the wide bend. If nothing else, Tara really knew how to pick a dramatic location to go with the already intense situation.

As the trail straightened out again, there was Tara, standing in a patch of sunlight about a hundred yards away. My pace quickened and there was a little bounce in my step as I approached her. She looked totally out of place with her flowing black hair, short black skirt and high heels. It was almost as if she were a fashion model who'd shown up for a 'business woman in the wilderness' shoot. She gave me a little wave. As I approached her my eyes flicked to her muscular legs for a moment. I realized just how much time she must spend either hiking some pretty steep paths or pounding away on the stair master. When I got to about twenty yards from her, I could see her lips set tight. Somehow her dancing, bright

almond eyes from before were narrower than I remembered..
She gave me a half-smile as I walked up to her.

"Thank you for coming out here, Ryan. I'm so sorry
about all this."

I nodded but wasn't sure what to say so just I waited
for Tara to continue.

"Three and a half years ago I met the two men who
took your daughter," she said looking at me with eyes as
serious as stone.

I folded my arms defensively across my chest and felt
my heart beating hard. Whatever way I'd been expecting the
conversation to start, this wasn't it.

"Their names are Alex and Jace. I don't know if
you paid any attention to them, but they were the two men
who sat down next to us when I met you at O'Malley's the
other night."

"The dark haired guy who looked like a middle
linebacker and the skinny blond one," I said.

"Yes. Jace is the blonde and a world class cyclist and
Alex actually *did* play linebacker in college for some small
school in Georgia. I first met them at a place called Sun Bar
in Chicago where a lot of six-figure professional types hang
out. Alex is also an attorney and Jace has his own optometrist
practice. Anyways, I was mentally in a rough spot at the
time. My divorce had flipped my life upside down and for
the first time in my life I'd felt vulnerable; unsure of who I
was or where I wanted to go. I had dated on and off since

my marriage had ended, but was struggling to connect with anyone – or even anything for that matter. My ex-husband had been a highly intense finance guy in Chicago and I'd just burnt out on the lifestyle and personalities we were hanging out with there,

But Jace and Alex were different."

Tara looked over at the forest, took a deep breath and let it out.

"Despite their professional success," she said looking back at me, "they weren't bogged down in the neurosis of the rat race. They were wealthy but relaxed, dated stunning women without being insecure players, and were very well versed in everything from classical music to martial arts to how to make world class tequila. Jace finishes in the top twenty in Iron Man Triathlons and Alex has a black belt in Jiu-Jitsu.

"And I soon found out, about a week after meeting them, they are both heavy into the occult."

"The occult?" I asked.

"Yeah, they'd actually met each other a couple of years prior in Jamaica. Both have a fascination with the darker side of things and the power that comes with it. When I'd met them I was dazzled by their confidence, their detachment from the stupid little trivialities of life. The three of us had money and we really started pushing the edge with learning about the magic of the unknown."

"And what were you finding?" I asked rubbing my arms. I felt a sudden chill and gray wisps of cloud had started to float under the blue sky.

"That there were ways beyond science and explanation to enhance your mind, to make yourself better than anyone else. Blending magic and the mind into one, so that with a simple wink of an eye you're bending impossibly rigid people to your will, understanding a foreign language the first time you hear it, and easily solving calculus problems in your head."

"Jesus," I said.

"Mm hmm," Tara said. "And then Jace got his hands on the big prize, something that instantly made everything else look like a complete waste of time. He'd gone to Russia by himself to check out some thousand-year-old texts and cracked onto something that only a handful of Uralic mystics had ever successfully obtained, immortality, – never grow old, never die. Jace brought the book back to Chicago and he and Alex got to work figuring it all out. It was complex, the most difficult spell they'd gotten involved with. And since I was busy with a big property case at the time, they did most of the work. But," Tara ran her hand through her hair, took a deep breath and let it out, "the essence of it required the capturing the soul of a young girl and harvesting her spirit. At first I didn't want anything to do with it, but Alex and Jace assured me the girl wouldn't be harmed – not permanently at least. Her soul would rejuvenate within her and we would use her original one to begin the process. From that point on, every three years we'd need a new soul and a new girl to stay immortal."

Tara took another pull of the cigarette and blew a wisp of smoke out. "At least that's how they explained it to me."

"And Jessica Ray?"

"Yes, Jessica was the first one. We came out to Gold Pine because of the privacy and the mountain. There was something about the presence of an external strength bonding with the internal that we were getting from the girl. Alex and Jace had taken her when they found her wandering by herself outside of town and took her to the abandoned warehouse that they'd secretly purchased through a third party. We performed the ceremony which involved a lot of chanting and a glowing green rock but it didn't just take the energy from Jessica, it drained her of her life all together."

"And now her empty spirit is trapped in the warehouse," I said.

"Yes. She can't move on and now she's stuck there. And while she's not an evil spirit, it's not who she was either. She's just lost now, gone. A taunting, twisted version of herself. After it was over, Alex and Jace admitted to me that they knew what would happen to her all along. They kept me in the dark because they needed me and loved me and they knew I wouldn't take part in the ceremony if I knew what the real end result would be."

"So why are you still here? Did you go to the sheriff? The police?"

"Alex and Jace told me that if I left town or went to the authorities they'd come after me. They also knew that since I'd been so closely involved, I'd most likely be implicated in her death as well. On top of all that, it would have been extremely difficult to prove. There were no witnesses, the girl was lost when Alex and Jace found her, and neither of them had any public connection to the warehouse. When they buried her the whole town showed up, and Alex and Jace, being the duplicitous bastards they are, actually brought flowers.

"And I stuck around hoping to be able to stop them before they took the next one."

"And Elyse is next," I said.

"That's right. Unless we stop them. Tonight."

I folded my arms and shook my head. It was crazy, but at this point it made perfect sense. "My dog, Oscar, two nights ago also vanished," I said. "Just ran off into the darkness outside the warehouse and I haven't seen him since."

Tara nodded and dropped the cigarette on the trail, rubbing it out with her foot. "It's possible he got lured into the ghost girl's realm and is now trapped there," she said.

I let out a nervous chuckle and looked off into the woods. Again, in this Twilight Zone nightmare it seemed totally understandable. "So what do we do?" I asked as I watched a raven land on a pine tree branch about fifty feet up. Was it the same one as before? It tilted its head and just stared at me.

"Alex and Jace are performing the ritual at midnight tonight. Meet me outside the warehouse at 11 o'clock. I'll let us inside. There should be some big boxes in there for us to take cover behind and I'll have a gun for you. When Alex and Jace show up we'll save your daughter." The raven flew off just as Tara checked her watch. "Okay, I have to get back to the office. Wait a good twenty minutes after I leave before you head back. I'll see you at eleven."

Tara walked off down the trail and I was alone.

It was now almost two o'clock.

I checked my phone for missed calls or messages and then I walked a little farther down the trail. The trees parted a bit more this way and I had a clear view of the mountain looming under the darkening sky like a big, gray overlord. I rubbed my chin and watched as thick strands of black cloud swirled over the monstrous piece of rock and thought about the idea of these selfish pricks using my daughter as some sort of spiritual power pack.

As I turned and started to walk back down the trail, the shadows got longer and the strip of sky turned completely gray. I broke into a fast jog and kept it up until I rejoined the road. Sticking my hands in my jean pockets, I walked with long, fast strides back towards town and about ten minutes later, stepped onto the sidewalk at the corner of the hotel.

After spending last night having been drugged and having had a gun aimed at my head, I figured I should lay low from this point on. The car still wouldn't be ready for a couple of days anyway and I didn't want to bump into the Deputy. Who knew how closely Alex or Jace – or anyone else – was watching me? They said I had until sundown to get out and after hearing Tara's story, I believed them. But I also knew it was most likely a case of them simply wanting me out of the way, and as long as I stayed in the hotel I should be safe.

I pulled open the hotel door and was welcomed by the customary smile and nod from Clare. Part of me wanted to talk to this nice stranger who had, in one sense been with me through this terrible ordeal, but I just returned the smile, said "hi," and went into the open elevator and back up to my room. I tossed the keys on the dresser, took off my shoes and shirt and laid down on the bed with my phone next to me. My legs and head felt heavy and as soon as I shut my eyes I drifted off to sleep.

When I woke up hours later Jessica Ray's ghost stood over my bed. Her blurry white body hovered a few inches above the covers as the light from the hotel sign lit the room in a dim yellow glow.

"Jessica," I said quietly.

Her eyes narrowed and she shot upwards as a blast of icy wind tore the covers off the bed and smacked them against the TV and dresser. I jumped up off the bed, switched the lights on and when I looked up at the ceiling she was gone.

The clock said 10:37 and I got the hell out of the room and went downstairs.

The lobby was dim and whoever was supposed to be at the desk right now wasn't there. It didn't matter anyway. I was about to either save my daughter or wind up buried in that cemetery. I pushed the door open and walked into the night to see Tara in a long leather coat with a flashlight in her hand standing at the corner of the warehouse. The rest of the street was deathly quiet.

"Are you ready, Ryan?" Tara asked as approached her.

"Yeah, let's get in there." I thought about mentioning the little visit Jessica Ray had just paid me but I didn't want to complicate something that was already on the edge.

Tara nodded and handed me the flashlight. She then reached into her purse and pulled out a handgun. "Do you know how to use this?" she asked.

"Yeah, it's a Glock, right? I've gone shooting before with my buddy who has one."

"Good, and yes, it's a Glock 17. Also, I didn't want to alarm you before, but you're going to have to go in alone. Let's just say Jessica Ray's ghost isn't too crazy about me and she could make things a lot more difficult for us in there."

I wasn't happy about Tara not coming in but based on what I'd already experienced with Jessica's spirit, I couldn't argue with her. "All right, I get that," I said, taking the gun.

We walked up to the door of the warehouse and Tara took a key out of her jacket pocket. "Haven't used this in three years. I don't think Alex and Jace even realize I still have it." She inserted the key into the padlock that secured the big heavy door. With a twist of the key and a loud click the latch popped open and Tara lifted the bolt. "I haven't been here for three years – since Jessica. So I have no idea what you'll find when you go in. Good luck."

"And where are you going to be?" I asked.

"I'll be around," she said as she leaned in and gave me a kiss on the cheek.

It had been a long time since I had any sort of intimate contact. Not since Nicole had died. And at a time like this, it felt strange to feel that small streak of excitement rush through me. Tara smiled, spun around and hurried off, disappearing a couple of seconds later around the side of the warehouse.

I stared at the handle for a long second and then pulled the door open. Thick musky air assaulted my senses, but I ignored it and peered inside. Other than streaks of white moonlight flowing in through the windows and a large stack of a few dozen chest-high boxes in the far right corner, it was just a cold barren room with a concrete floor and about a dozen dome shaped light fixtures hanging from the ceiling. I stepped forward and closed the door behind me.

So this was a ghost girl's prison.

The fuzzy lights of the homes outside of town glittered through the far windows and I looked around the room. The boxes would be good cover to wait for Alex and Jace, and once they were here I could use the Glock any way I'd have to.

As a gleam of purple shined in the corner of my eye, I knew it was coming from Jessica Ray's tombstone, and I looked through the windows to see the ghostly light bursting out of the cemetery. At this point, I'd seen enough weirdness that my heart stayed calm and my hands remained steady. I walked to the back of the warehouse and placed my fingertips on the windows as I peered through. "What are you up to, little girl?" I whispered.

Just as if an Arctic front had blown into the warehouse, a thick wall of icy-cold pressed against my back, and I turned around.

My heart started to race.

Jessica Ray stood in the center of the room. Her blue dress glowed bright against her faded white body and those narrow gray eyes coldly staring, locked onto me.

"Jesus, what did they do to you?" I quietly asked.

Her arm flashed out like a laser and her cold, wispy hand wrapped around my wrist so tightly that my hand popped open and the flashlight fell out, hitting the cement with a crack and going dark. I tried to pull my arm away but her strong grip held it still. Icy panic shot through my bones as Jessica stared at me with her wide, dead eyes. She took a step closer and the air in the warehouse became thick and wavy as if a gas furnace had been turned on too high. The ceiling lamps started to burn white-hot bright, spastically flashing like drunken strobe lights.

In the center of the warehouse, the blurred, scratched-out images of Alex holding a still living Jessica Ray as Jace and Tara looked on, materialized within the stomach-churning light show like some kind of hologram from the 1940s. Tara's face was tight and concerned while Alex and Jace looked like they were filled with excited anticipation. As Jessica Ray struggled to pull out of Alex's tight-armed grasp, Jace slid a knife out of his long, black coat, held it over her chest and started to recite a kind of choppy, ancient sounding language. Tara's face twisted in horror as she grabbed Jace's arm, but he shoved her to the ground. Jessica's scream was deafeningly loud, like a high-speed drill. Jace then plunged the knife into her chest. Her body went limp and Alex let her slide to the ground. With the knife back inside his coat he took a glowing purple stone out of his pocket, holding it over her head while again speaking in that bizarre language. Gold light swirled out of the lifeless corpse a few seconds later, floating halfway to the ceiling and then shooting into the bodies of all three living attendants.

And then the lights stopped flashing, the air went back to normal and the images of the death ritual sparked and fizzled into nothingness.

The cold pressure around my wrist was gone, and so was Jessica Ray.

Staggering to the side of the warehouse, I slumped down behind the boxes and shut my eyes. The screams, the lights, Jessica's freezing ghostly hand. It felt like every one of my senses had been hit by a freight train and my eyelids were heavy. Darkness washed over me as my body seemed to want to shut down.

I was jolted out of my daze by the high-pitched sound of keys rattling outside the warehouse door. It was as if someone had thrown a bucket of ice in my face. This was it. I double-checked that I was obscured behind the boxes as I heard the clicking of the lock and the sharp thud of the latch being set against the door. The door creaked open and Elyse walked in with Alex's heavy hands on her shoulders and Jace following closely behind them. Jace shut the door and I watched as Alex guided my daughter to the exact same spot where Jessica's vision showed me her death had occurred. Elyse's body trembled as tears streamed down her face. Jace in the same long, black coat, quick-stepped past them to the windows, stared out for a few seconds, and then turned and stepped up to my daughter.

I shot around the boxes and pointed the gun at Jace. "Let her go," I said.

Alex's grip tightened causing Elyse to wince and Jack put up his hands. "Not bad, Ryan. Let me guess, Tara let you in here?"

I walked towards him with the gun aimed at his head and stopped in the center of the warehouse.

"Move that hand another inch and you brain is going to get a very bad case of lead poisoning," I said. "Now Alex, you're going to let go of my daughter or you and your friend are going to become permanent residents of this place."

"Come on now, Ryan," Alex said as he began to walk Elyse towards me, "we both know you're no killer, and you're right, we don't need your daughter. There's plenty of other girls out there. So let's just call this a simple misunderstanding and everyone can go their separate ways."

I saw Jace start to move towards me and as I looked back over at him, Alex shoved Elyse to the ground and dove shoulder first into my ribs, knocking the gun out of my hands and driving me to the concrete. In a flash he scrambled on top of me, slammed his fist into my nose, then grabbed the neck of my shirt to lift me to my feet. I watched Jace pick up my gun as lightning bolts of pain shot through my face and the ground felt like I was trying to stand on a carnival moonwalk.

Elyse was sitting on her knees crying, when Alex snatched her wrist and pulled her off the ground.

"Like I said before, Ryan, it was a first-time last-time offer," Jace said as he raised the gun to my head. A blur of sharp teeth, snarls and fur flew out of thin air onto Jace and he screamed as Oscar bit into his neck. I grabbed Jace's hand and ripped the gun away, shooting Alex twice in the chest. Jace managed to throw Oscar off him and charged at me screaming. I pulled the trigger again. This time I aimed for his head. His body snapped back. His arms flew into the air like an electrified ragdoll and he landed on his back with his legs spread and his head tilted to the side.

Elyse ran up to me and I knelt down, setting the gun on the concrete, as she wrapped her arms around my back. "I was so scared, daddy!" she cried. "They kept me locked in the basement and told me they were going to cut me open and…and…" she couldn't get the words out as tears streamed down her cheeks.

"It's okay, honey. I know. Everything's going to be all right now," I said as I stroked the back of her head and Oscar nuzzled his face into my stomach. I looked over at Alex laying face-first on the ground in a pool of blood and then over at Jace who was sprawled out like a scarecrow knocked off its frame. "Immortals no more," I whispered.

"My God, Ryan, you did it," a honey-like voice echoed across the warehouse.

I hadn't even heard the door open and looked over to see Tara sauntering towards us. Her hips swaying as her heels clicked against the hard floor. "Thank you so much," she said as she reached into her purse, took a gun out and aimed it at me.

Oscar snarled and started to move towards her.

"Stay Oscar," I said.

The yellow lab stopped walking but a low growl still rumbled out of him.

"What is this, Tara?" I asked.

Keeping the gun locked on me she sidestepped over to Jace's body, reached into his coat and took out a long black knife.

"Well, it's like this, Ryan," she said looking over the knife, "one thing I forgot to mention to you earlier is that despite my initial dismay at Jessica Ray's death, I've become quite accustomed to, and extremely happy with, being immortal. No more fear, no more worry, consequences become irrelevant." She stood up with the gun in one hand pointed at me and the knife in the other. "And I can do things that no one else on the planet dares do."

"Like climb big mountains," I said with a half a smirk.

"Oh, I've already done a lot better than that," Tara said. "However, immortality is a very long time. And the prospect of being stuck for eternity with these two womanizing idiots was a little too much to bear. Even the best mates get tiresome and those nasty threats they made after Jessica's Ray's death never wore off. I got rid of my first husband because he was a manipulating S.O.B. and now, thanks to you, these two are history also." She stepped up to Elyse with the gun still pointed at me. "Come over here, pumpkin."

"Don't do it, Elyse," I said setting my hand over the Glock.

"Get down on your knees or I'm going to shoot your daddy in the face," she said in her silky smooth voice.

Elyse got up and Tara guided her with the gun until she was almost at the corner of the warehouse. "Get down on your knees, dear," she said.

Elyse put one knee onto the concrete floor and then another.

"Good girl," Tara said, "this won't hurt a bit." She held the knife in front of her face and began chanting in the same dialect that Jace had spouted in the vision Jessica had shown me. Tara's body started to tremble and as her voice became louder and higher pitched, it lost its beauty and she sounded like a demented preacher. She raised the knife and a screaming flash of white and blue whipped around her face, causing her to drop the gun as she swatted at the ghost girl. Tara grabbed Elyse by the throat with her free hand and I snatched the Glock off the ground and fired three bullets into her just as she plunged the knife downward. Tara collapsed on the concrete in a bloody heap and I ran over to Elyse and picked her up. She held onto the back of my neck and I scratched Oscar's head as he pressed himself against my leg.

As I stared at our reflection in the window, a blur of blue and white appeared next to me and I looked over to see Jessica Ray smiling up at me with happy bright eyes. We looked at each other for a second and then she spun into a gold ray of light, shot through the window, and flew off into the starlit black sky. I stepped up to the window and set my palm on the glass. Nicole was still gone and my financial career might be over, but for the first time since this had all begun I felt a surge of warmth and brightness for the future. My daughter loved me and we would build a new life from here.

"Time to go, guys," I said as I set Elyse down and gave Oscar a pat on the head.

I then took my daughter's hand and the three of us walked through the warehouse and out into the Gold Pine night.

OTHER BOOKS AVAILABLE FROM PARANORMAL PUBLISHING

Ghost Girl Gone
A Paranormal Mystery Thriller, Books One,
Two, Three, and the Boxed Set.

True Ghost Stories and Hauntings
Chilling Stories of Poltergeists, Unexplained
Phenomenon, and Haunted Houses
Volumes I, II, III, IV, V, and Boxed Set of Volumes 1-III.

For kids: *Ghost Coloring Book*

Kids love coloring these ghosts as they bring them to life. Let your imagination fly and have lots of fun with this spooky activity book!

DID YOU ENJOY THIS BOOK?

If you enjoyed reading this book, please consider leaving a positive review on Amazon so others might find it. If there was something you believe needed changing or you didn't like, please email the publisher with your comments at Publisher@paranormalpublishing.net

BONUS FOR READERS OF THIS BOOK

Get 3 FREE ghost stories at
www.paranormalpublishing.com/ghoststories

ABOUT THE AUTHOR

Simon B. Murik. Simon is the son of a long line of mediums and sensitives originally from Eastern Europe. At a very early age Simon realized he had a connection with the other side and his family helped him develop those capacities and gifts. Today people seek him out to share their paranormal encounters and seek his help in making sense of these experiences.

Simon's writing is inspired by other's stories as well as by his own occult experiences and his muse. In addition to Ghost Girl Gone, Simon is the primary author and editor of True Ghost Stories and Hauntings, Volumes 1-V. Look for more books by Simon which are published exclusively by Paranormal Publishing.